"'The Mystery of the Magic' will take you on fun adventure ride. Escape with Luce, his fairy friend, and the king of the land on their quest for a portal that doesn't want to be found. You'll be swept away in the world Mantler has woven in this latest instalment of the Kings of Proster." -Julie Howard

The Mystery of the Magic

B. Heather Mantler

Mantler Publishing Prince George

ISBN:192750712X
ISBN-13:9781927507124

Library and Archives Canada Cataloguing in Publication

Mantler, B. Heather, 1987-, author
The mystery of the magic / B. Heather Mantler.

ISBN 978-1-927507-12-4 (pbk.)

I. Title.

PS8626.A676M97 2014 C813'.6 C2014-901201-2

To those whose names and descriptions appear in this book. I apologize if the personalities do not match.

LUCE SHOWS UP IN PROSTER TO ASK KING DRISCOLL FOR HELP IN HIS QUEST

Luce shifted from shadow to shadow as he walked through the capital of Proster toward the castle and the current residence of the king. He stopped at one of the cross streets near the market place as he waited for the patrol to go passed. They did not even glance in his direction, but walked passed him as if he was one of the shadows. The patrol reached the next cross street.

Luce was about to cross the street and keep going when there was a squeak from inside his pocket. The patrol was too far way to hear it. Luce opened his cloak. A small head popped up out of the inside pocket of his cloak. The fairy's head glowed in the dark so the thick and curly strawberry blonde hair and pale face with sharp but delicate features were visible.

"Are we there yet?" the fairy's voice was high with a bit of a squeak, "It is stifling in here."

"A little further," Luce answered.

"Okay," the fairy said before disappearing back into the pocket. Luce checked around. The patrol was off in the distance. Luce continued on. He crossed the road and back into the shadows.

"So, your friend Zebulon will help us?" the fairy said from inside Luce's pocket.

"Zebulon is dead," Luce answered, "Has been for twenty-five years. We are looking for help from his son, Driscoll."

"Will Driscoll help us?" the fairy asked.

"I hope so," Luce answered.

"What did he die of?" the fairy asked.

"Who?" Luce asked.

"Zebulon," the fairy said.

"Stomach problems," Luce answered, "But it took two years to kill him. Driscoll has been king since Zebulon got sick. All we need to do is identify ourselves as Zebulon's friends and then hopefully he'll help us with our quest."

"And if he does not?" the fair asked.

"We will have to find some other way to get the information and help," Luce answered, "But Driscoll was very much attached to his father, so we should not have a problem."

"His father has been dead for years," the fairy said, "Why would being his friend mean anything now?"

"It will," Luce said. The fairy didn't say anything as they continued.

Luce reached the gates to the courtyard. All three of them were open. Through the main one, Luce could see multiple carriages waiting with drivers huddled in a group to one side.

"Something is happening in the castle," Luce said, "We are not likely to be able to sneak in."

"What are you going to do?" the fairy asked.

"Go through the front door," Luce answered, "We will need the castle steward to find Driscoll anyway."

"Be careful," the fairy said.

Luce stepped out into the street and let the shadows melt away from him. The sound of his boots on the stone of the street echoed in the dark and empty space. He walked through the gate without being challenged, but then there were no guards around. In the court yard, the drivers looked up at him, but they did not bother him. It was not their job to protect the castle and the cloak he wore was expensive enough that he was likely invited. They went back to their conversation. Luce never stopped. He went around the carriage in front of the door. When he reached the door itself, Luce knocked.

It was less than a minute before the door opened and the castle steward stood there looking at Luce. At first he seemed to wonder why Luce did not come in, then he realized Luce was not here for whatever event was happening.

"Is there something I can help you with?" the castle steward asked.

"I need to speak with King Driscoll," Luce answered.

"He is busy celebrating his birthday with a masquerade ball," the castle steward said.

"It should only take a few minutes of his time," Luce said, "Then I have to be on my way."

"Very well, I will go ask him," the castle steward said, "You can wait in here."

Luce stepped inside and the castle steward closed the door. The castle steward then went around him and down the hallway. He went into the open doorway at the end.

Luce stayed where he was. From there he could hear the music coming from the doorway and see people going passed in various costumes. All of them were wearing masks. Luce wondered briefly if his request would give away which one was the king.

"Well?" the fairy asked from inside Luce's pocket.

"A while longer," Luce whispered back.

"This pocket stinks," the fairy said, "You need to get your cloak cleaned more often."

"Hopefully you will not have to spend much time in there after this," Luce whispered.

The castle steward came back through the doorway. No one followed him out. Luce waited until the castle steward reached him.

"His majesty is willing to meet you in his study," the castle steward said, "Follow me."

Luce nodded. The castle steward turned and headed back down the hallway. Luce followed. There were two hallways branching off just before the entrance to the throne room. No one inside seemed to have been bothered by anything happening. The castle steward went down the hallway on the left. They went along this hallway for a while, until it came to another hallway that connected to this one. They turned down this hallway and went to the end. At the end there was a closed door and a staircase. The castle steward knocked on the door before opening it. The castle steward held the door for Luce, who stepped into the office. Once he was inside the castle steward closed the door.

The king stood behind his desk. The mask only covered the area around his eyes, leaving the very natural beard beneath it visible. Above the mask was hair the same brown as the beard with a golden crown placed on top of it. The coat was a deep purple with matching leggings and shoes. The trimmings were gold to match the crown. It was easy to identify that he was the king even with the mask on. The man himself was a foot shorter than Luce, but that still made him a good six inches taller than his father had been, though he was slightly narrower in the shoulders and chest.

"The steward said you wished to talk to me," Driscoll said.

"Yes," Luce said, "My name is Luce and I was a friend of your father, Zebulon."

A sad expression flickered in those blue eyes, but it was gone very quickly.

"Of course," Driscoll said, "Any friend of my father's is welcome."

"The last time I saw your father I told him about a quest I was on," Luce said, "And he told me that should I ever need assistance, I could get help for him. Unfortunately I need help, but your father is no longer here to help me."

"If my father promised you help, I will do what I can to help you," Driscoll said with a smile, "What is it that you require help with?"

"I have been searching for where the magic went," Luce said, "Because before I visited the kingdom the first time, the magic from this part of the world had disappeared. I had asked Zebulon about it, but he did not know anything. There was a portal from which the magic was coming into this area. Something happened to the portal and I need help finding it. The problem is that no one seems to know where the portal was, except King Proster. I thought he might have left some information on it."

"I believe there is some information on it somewhere," Driscoll said turning to look at the shelves behind him, "I am not sure where it is at this time though." Driscoll turned back to Luce.

"Perhaps you could find it tomorrow," Luce said, "Sometime after you have recovered from the party."

"Of course," Driscoll said, "I will have the steward make up rooms for you."

"As long as there are two," the fairy squeaked from inside Luce's pocket.

"Who is that?" Driscoll asked. Luce opened his cloak and let the fairy out of his pocket. She spread her green wings and then fluttered them to keep herself in the air. She was wearing a green dress stitched together from leaves and fairy magic.

"This is Sandra," Luce said, "I found her in my travels. She had ended up on the wrong side of the portal and now cannot get back. I promised to find a way to get her home."

"Wow," Driscoll stared at Sandra in wonderment, "I have never seen anything like her before."

"Fairies are very rare on this side of the portal," Sandra said, "On the other side there are whole cities of fairies."

"That would be amazing to see," Driscoll said, "Never in my lifetime have I ever seen anything like that."

"I do not live in the cities," Sandra said, "They are too crowded. I am a forest fairy and we do not like crowded places."

"Then I will make sure to mention to the steward that there needs to be two rooms made up," Driscoll said, "Is there anything you need, specifically in yours?"

"Supper," Sandra answered, "We have been traveling all day without much rest and lunch was rationed. We did not stop for supper."

"I will make sure he sends supper up for both of you," Driscoll said.

"Thank you," Luce bowed.

"Anything for my father's friend," Driscoll said with a smile, "Come down after lunch and I will see if I can find the information."

"We will see you then," Luce said before bowing again and opening the door. He stepped out and Sandra followed him. The castle steward was waiting outside. He went inside when Driscoll called him.

"Do you have enough magic to make yourself invisible until we reach the room?" Luce asked Sandra.

"Not today," Sandra answered, "But I do not want to go back in that pocket of yours."

"Then we just have to hope we do not meet anyone who is going to question your appearance or wish to do anything bad to you," Luce said.

"I know human's response to fairies," Sandra said as she settled on Luce's shoulder, "I am just hoping we do not meet anyone who might notice me."

The castle steward closed the door on his way out of the office. He looked at Luce and briefly glanced at Sandra.

"This way," the castle steward said before turning and heading down the hallway. Luce glanced at the stairway, but followed the castle steward.

The castle steward opened the door to a guest suite. There were four rooms total in the suite. Three of them were bedrooms and the fourth was a sitting room. Sandra took off to look the bedrooms over as Luce glanced back at the castle steward.

"Is there anything in particular you wish to eat?" the castle steward asked.

"Whatever is leftover is fine," Luce answered.

"I will have it sent up immediately," the castle steward said before leaving. Luce closed the door behind him. Luce thought about putting a protection spell on it, but decided that he should wait until after the food had been delivered. There was limited energy to create the spell and wasting it was not a good idea. The castle was probably the safest place in Proster, but that did not mean there were no dangers.

"This is my room," Sandra said from the doorway to the right.

"That is fine," Luce said, "Food should be here shortly."

"We are going to have a problem with Driscoll," Sandra said, "He had that look."

"I saw it," Luce said, "But he is willing to help us and we need that help."

"What about his insistence to come with us?" Sandra asked.

"We will let him," Luce answered, "He will not be a problem to us. We can even use his help. He has the maps and some of the information we need, not to mention he is likely to be a good fighter. All of which is useful to us."

"He will want to go through the portal," Sandra said, "Most humans who go inside mess things up there. We cannot let him go through."

"The portal guardian will decide who is okay to get through," Luce said, "Most likely he will not allow Driscoll through."

"The portal guardian when I went through did not care who he let through," Sandra said, "But the portal guardian has probably changed since then. Otherwise the magic would still be the same as it was before. Whether the new one will let him through or not, I don't know. But him being there is a bad idea."

"We will sort that out when we get that far," Luce said, "We are still in the city and he has not asked to go with us. He might have something that keeps him here and will demand to be brought back the information as to what happened. His father would have never had any interest in going."

"Driscoll and his father are not the same person," Sandra said, "You have not been here in twenty-five years, lots of things could have changed. Driscoll could be nothing like his father."

"How about we discuss this again when Driscoll asks to come with us," Luce said, "Until then we worry about getting the information we need to find the portal."

"Okay," Sandra said, "But if he does come with us, you have to keep him from entering the portal and doing damage in my world."

"I will do my best," Luce said.

There was a knock on the door. Luce opened it. A servant stood there with a tray of food.

"As requested, sir," the servant said.

"Put it on the table," Luce said.

"Yes, sir," the servant said. He entered the room, placed the tray on the table, and then scurried from the room as if he was scared to stay. Luce closed the door.

"Do you always have that effect on people?" Sandra asked as she set herself down on the table next to the tray.

"Mostly on servants," Luce said, "Though on some others as well. It usually works in my favour." Luce sat down on the chair closest to the table. They both started to eat.

When Sandra was full, she flew to the room she picked out. The door closed most of the way behind her. Luce finished most of the rest of what was on the tray before going to the door. He put the protection spell on it before going into the room farthest from the one picked by Sandra. He put his cloak on the chair before sitting down on the bed. Luce crossed his legs, rested his hands on his knees, and closed his eyes. He repeatedly whispered something under his breath until he was in a trance. This helped him gather as much energy from things around him as he could. Eventually his head fell to his chest and he was asleep.

The curtains over the windows were heavy and kept the room in darkness even though Luce could feel the sun had risen. He stretched and got up off the bed. Going to the window he opened the curtains and looked out at the pink sky. There was nothing like a sunrise when a person had time to enjoy it, rather than having to press on.

Luce pushed the window open and was greeted with the coldness of a fall morning. It was likely the first frost of the season. It made Luce glad he had a bed and room in the castle rather than having to sleep on the ground under a tree somewhere. If he still had the prestige of being the ambassador of Wodend he would never have to do such things, but since the takeover of Wodend by Lithimin there was nothing. He no longer had a king or country. It was now called Menano and the king was the old royalty of Lithimin, which had a long and renowned line.

Luce had been at the ocean and had not been able to get back to save anything, even his parent's estate. Zebulon had wanted to send troops to help, but word reached him too late. There was nothing anyone would do about the invasion and there was no one rising up to put the old family on the throne because there was no one left from it. The nobility had all been wiped out, except for Luce. No one had time to run or send their children away. They were all dead. This meant Luce had no home, no king, no money, and no support. And as much as he longed for all of that back, there was nothing he could do about it.

Maybe that was why he had taken Sandra in when he had found her. He figured she was in the same position as he was. She had been trapped in this world when the magic disappeared. She had been losing energy since then and when Luce had found her she was just about completely out of energy. She probably would have been dead in a couple more days. He had to teach her ways of gathering her energy from her surroundings. She was used to doing it unconsciously, but with so little energy she now had to practice doing it consciously. Fortunately she was a good student and she now had enough energy to survive as well as do small amounts of magic.

There was a knock at the door to the suite. Luce closed the window before turning and going to the door. He stopped and took down the protection spell before opening the door. The same servant from last night was there with a new tray of food. Luce stepped aside and let the servant in. The servant went to the table and set down the new tray before picking up the old tray.

"Has other people gotten up yet?" Luce asked before the servant could rush out.

"Some," the servant answered, "But not many. It was expected."

"Is his majesty awake?" Luce asked.

"I do not know," the servant answered, "He has not been seen, if he is awake."

"Thank you," Luce said. The servant hurried passed him and out the door. Luce closed it behind him before taking a seat and started breakfast. Sandra did not come out of her room. Luce thought about waking her, but decided not to. The meeting was not until after lunch and he would leave enough food for her in case she got up before lunch was brought up to them.

When Luce was finished eating he went back to the bedroom. This time he sat down in the chair and took out his badly beaten spell book. He opened it and started to read the spells. If he reinforced the memory of the spells they were far more likely to come to mind when he needed them and he would not get any parts wrong in the reciting of them.

Luce was deep in his reading when there came another knock on the door. He put away his spell book before getting to his feet. He went to the door and opened it. This time it was the castle steward with a tray of food.

"Good morning," the castle steward said with a nod.

"Good morning," Luce said as he stepped out of the way for the castle steward to pass him.

"King Driscoll asked to make sure that you remembered your appointment with him today after lunch," the castle steward said as he set down the tray he was carrying and picked up the other.

"I remember," Luce said.

"He also wondered if there was anything you needed that had not already been provided," the castle steward asked.

"No, everything is fine," Luce answered, "If there was anything else needed I would mention it."

"Very good, sir," the castle steward said before giving a small bow and leaving the room. Luce closed the door behind. Sandra had not come out yet, so Luce went to the door and knocked on it.

"Yes?" Sandra's voice was sleepy.

"Lunch is here," Luce answered, "And then our meeting with the king."

"I will be out in a minute," Sandra called back.

Luce sat down and started to eat. Sandra came out a minute later and joined Luce. They did not speak as we ate.

They had just finished when there was a knock at the door. Luce went into the bedroom and put his cloak on. Going back into the sitting room, Luce found Sandra still sitting on the table.

"Are you going to turn yourself invisible?" Luce asked her, "Or ride in my cloak pocket?"

"There is less magical energy to gather here than

anywhere else we have been," Sandra said, "I have not been able to gather enough to turn myself invisible for long enough to get to the king's study. So, I have to ride in your pocket."

Luce opened his cloak and Sandra slipped into his pocket. The knock came again. This time Luce opened the door. In the hallway stood a young woman. She was almost as tall as Luce and she had more muscle than fat, but it was all lean muscle. Her flawless skin was like a deep tan, but it could only be her natural skin colour. Her face was thin with slight points on her ears and the most beautiful hazel eyes.

"My name is Rana," the young woman said with a slight curtsy, "His majesty, King Driscoll, asked if I would escort you as the castle steward is currently busy with something else."

"I am Luce," Luce replied, "Lead the way."

Rana smiled and Luce smiled back. Rana started down the hallway. Luce closed the door behind himself before following her. Rana wore a light pink dress which had a neckline that was high enough to be modest and low enough to keep a man interested. The bust might not be as large as some at court, but it fit her figure. Her dress reached the top of her shoes, but did not impede her walking.

"So, what position in court do you hold that has you escorting guests?" Luce asked.

"I am an advisor to whoever sits on the throne," Rana answered.

"And what did you do to gain such a position?" Luce asked.

"My mother was consort to King Driscoll before she died," Rana answered.

"But he is not your father?" Luca asked.

"Unknown to everyone, she was pregnant with me and my brother before they married," Rana answered, "But he raised us as his own."

"Then the heir is your half-brother?" Luce asked.

"No," Rana answered, "Prince Hillel is not related to us by blood in any way, but King Driscoll treats us all as his children. My brother, Weldon, and I have been given the title of advisors to the throne. Though we hardly are able to give King Driscoll any advice, but we do other things for him. Since he could have thrown us out, or done worse, I am grateful for everything he has done."

"He seems to be a great man and a good king," Luce said.

"He has his faults, just as everyone else," Rana said, "However, his good out weighs the bad. The people like him and he keeps saying that is all that matters."

"He is right," Luce said, "A king who is liked by the people is very important, but it also matters that the king does the best he can for his people."

"Very true," Rana said. They had reached the door to King Driscoll's office. Rana knocked on the door. There was a call from inside inviting them to enter. Rana opened the door and bowed.

"Luce is here as requested," Rana said.

"Thank you," Driscoll answered, "He may come in." Luce entered the study. He watched Rana leave. She met his eyes once and then was gone, closing the door behind her. Luce turned to King Driscoll. Driscoll was wearing a boring brown and green outfit today. He did not have any jewellery on today, except a couple rings. His desk was covered with various papers with two books set on top of it all.

"I hope you had a good night," Driscoll said.

"Very good," Luce said, "It had been a while since I have felt the comfort of clean sheets and it was wonderful."

"I am glad you enjoyed it," Driscoll said, "I have spent the morning looking for the information you need. All I could find are these two books from my grandfather. Both of them talk about various magical beasts. I can find only a brief mention of the portal in one of them, but it says nothing about the location of the portal. The map that I was sure was there seems to have disappeared."

"Could it be somewhere else in the castle?" Luce asked.

"I looked through the library," Driscoll answered, "Nothing has been moved from the study up there and I could find nothing like the map. However, after my search I remember a man who came through a year ago. He was here to sell what he could to who he could and his targets were the nobles. The man gained much from them and wandered places he should not have gone. The guards found him a few places he should not have been before it was brought to my attention. I ordered his bags searched and everything returned to their proper places, but I believe some things still disappeared with him. I thought it would be okay to kick him out of the kingdom and swear to cut of his hands if he should ever show himself again. But if he has the map then I fear I was wrong to let him leave."

"You did not know at the time," Luce said, "Best to accept the past and let us move on. Does the passage from the book make mention of which direction we are most likely to find the portal?"

"No," Driscoll answered, "But I have been told that it lies in the forest if a person goes left when they reach the city gates. The distance, or where in the forest, I do not have that information."

"That is a good start," Luce said, "Much better than I had found so far."

"That forest is large and very dense," Driscoll said, "Unless you have some way of locating the portal you could be lost for a very long time."

"There is no way of locating the portal through magic," Luce said, "Even if I had the energy for the spell, it seems that the closer to the portal I get there is less energy of which to gather. The portal was the source of magic in this area and now there is no magic here. Any magical energy which is farther away enters this world from other portals. I have gone searching for others, but no one wishes to help me in such a quest. And as one without kingdom, it is hard to get help, or be allowed to stay any place."

"You are from Wodend?" Driscoll asked, "I thought none of the nobility survived."

"None that were in the kingdom at the time did," Luce answered, "I was on my quest and all others had been called home. I did not receive the call home until after the takeover was complete. Since there is no one left to retake the kingdom, I live landless and without aid in my quest."

"Then it is even more important I help you with your quest," Driscoll said, "Even if I gave you a place in my kingdom, you would have no power. Asking a man to give up his trade is not something I believe to be a moral thing, even if it seems like a good idea for some."

"I appreciate that," Luce said, "The information will be useful in my quest."

"I was going to ask you a favour in return for this information," Driscoll said.

"Ask," Luce said.

"All my life I have lived in this city," Driscoll said, "Aside from some brief visits to a country estate, there has no chance for me to leave. My request is to merely be allowed to join you on your quest as you look through the forest for the portal. As much as I wish to enter it, that is not my place in this world. However, to hunt for it and see its form in this world would be a great delight. My kingdom will be fine during my leave because Hillel needs to learn the duties of a king. Since I expect to only stay away for a short while, he will be able to learn while I can still teach him the lessons from the mistakes he makes. The trip will do him good as well as myself. He is sure of himself, but lacks other necessities of a king. This time could teach him much and hopefully when I come back I can show him ways in which he can be a better king.

"I will not live forever and I want to know that my son will rule the kingdom the best way possible. There is nothing more dear to my heart than that. However, he needs space to learn. So, my request is that I may come with two of my guards to help you search the forest for the portal."

"That request I can grant," Luce said, "But I caution that you be careful about your heart and the temptation to not come back."

"I understand your concern," Driscoll said, "I know there is the temptation to go through the portal and see all the wonders which reside on the other side, but I also know my son still needs guidance. There is also the knowledge that I belong on this side of the portal."

"As long as you remember that," Luce said.

"You have my word," Driscoll said, "I will not give into the temptation. I will do everything in my power to come back."

"Very well," Luce said, "How long will it take you to get ready to leave?"

"Two days," Driscoll said, "I have not told anyone of my plan to leave, in case you said no. I will start the preparations as soon as the castle steward is done talking to the cook. If there is anything which you need to be supplied with, let me know so I can arrange it."

"There is nothing I can think of that I need," Luce said, "As long as you bring enough food for everyone who is coming."

"Of course," Driscoll said.

"I have another request of my own," Luce said.

"Ask," Driscoll said.

"The tallest tower of this castle has a room, which was the residence of a wizard at one time," Luce said, "I wish to go up there and look over the room. See if there is anything that might be useful to my quest."

"I know little about the tower room," Driscoll said, "Only that my grandfather sealed it off to prevent anyone from going in there and messing with things they did not understand. However, you are likely to understand it, so it might be much more appropriate for you to look around up there. There has been some push from people for me to clean out the room and put it to good use. Perhaps you can go through and determine what is dangerous while you wait for me to be ready. If you can make it easier to clean out, I would appreciate it. Anything you find that you can use, you are allowed to keep."

"Thank you," Luce said.

"The castle steward should be finished dealing with the cook shortly," Driscoll said, "He will already be concerned about the short notice of the trip. I need to speak with him."

"Of course," Luce said, "I should not detain you any longer," Luce gave Driscoll a bow before leaving the study. Once the door was closed behind him, Luce started up the nearby stairway. He opened his cloak and let Sandra out as he went up. She flew out of his pocket and landed on his shoulder.

"Well, that is settled," Sandra said, "Where are we headed?"

"The tower room," Luce said, "It could take a while to go through everything in there, so I might as well get started."

"Do you think he can keep temptation as bay when he is standing there before the portal?" Sandra asked.

"I do not know," Luce said, "But I believe that he will try to do so."

"I guess that is good enough for now," Sandra replied, "Though I would watch him and remind him of his promise once we are there. The portal can be hypnotizing to those unprepared for it."

"We will have to be the ones prepared for it," Luce said.

Sandra did not say anything else as Luce kept going up the stairs. The long travels mean Luce never tired as he went up the long staircase. He reached the top without so much as a laboured breath.

The window was there and showed the city below.

There was more dust on the sill than the last time Luce had been there. The bar was still over the door with the symbol marked on it. But the bar had been moved during the period since he had last been there. Luce frowned at it and placed his hand near the bar.

"Something wrong?" Sandra asked.

"Yes," Luce said, "Someone has been in there since it was barred."

"Who would have disobeyed the symbol?" Sandra asked.

"One who does not know what it means," Luce said, "Or someone who knows what it means, but does not care."

Luce slowly slipped the bar out of its place. He put it to one side before pulling the door open. Nothing happened, so Luce pulled it the rest of the way open and looked inside. There was a lot of destruction of items, but it did not look like it had been searched.

"Be careful," Sandra said before Luce stepped inside. He stepped around all debris. There was a table that had been overturned and everything that had been on it was now in pieces on the floor. There were several burn marks on the walls and floor. To one side was a skeleton in wizard's robes. Most of a skeleton, anyway. The skull was missing.

"Why take the skull?" Sandra asked.

"Because it is a powerful token that people are willing to pay for," Luce said, "A wizard's skull is a very powerful talisman, though it has no magical properties itself. It looks like the person who broke in took the skull."

"Maybe it was the man that King Driscoll was talking about," Sandra said, "The one who might have taken the map."

"A map showing where the portal is and the skull of a wizard," Luce said, "This man sounds like someone we should watch out for."

"But he has been gone a year," Sandra said, "He may have already be a large distance from here and we may never find him."

"Likely he is headed for the portal just as we are," Luce said, "Which is where we are likely to find him. He has had a year to get ahead of us, but we have no idea if there is anything that slowed him down. We can hope there was plenty to do so."

"In the meantime, is there anything in here you can use or is dangerous?" Sandra asked.

"It is all dead," Luce said, "There is no feeling of magic in this room. If there was anything magical here, whatever cut off the magic to everything else has made sure anything magical here is useless. There is no danger in here, unless you hit something with a sharp edge. But I am going to check everything anyway."

"I am going to go sit by the window in the outer room and look over the city," Sandra said, "I will catch a ride with you on your way down."

"Very well," Luce said, "Enjoy the view." Sandra flew out of the room. Luce turned his attention to the rest of the room. It was a mess and there was lots of damage. Overall it looked like there had been a fight in here, which was quite likely based on the hole and blood on the wizard's robe.

Luce tiptoed through this mess and looked for other rooms. There was only one door, which was covered by a curtain. Luce pushed the curtain aside and opened the door. The protection spells were thick enough that Luce could taste them. He stepped out of the room for a moment as he prepared a counter spell. Only once it was ready in his mind did he step back into the room. Luce muttered it as he waved his left hand in a circle that went above his head. There was a sizzling sound and slight sparkling as the spell dissipated.

Luce still felt another protection spell. He stepped farther into the room, but nothing stopped him or did him harm. Luce took another step, being a bit more careful this time. His toe reached a solid, but invisible wall. He reached out with his hand and touched it. It felt like a solid wall to his fingers, but the magic tickled all up his arm. Luce drew back from it. He briefly went through what spells would take something like that down. Finally he settled on one and reviewed it in his mind. When he was sure it was ready, he spoke it out loud while using both hands to create the circle. Green flames appeared, at first they did not seem to do anything, Then it was like whole walls were burning down, but nothing else in the room was touched.

Luce waited until the flames had disappeared. Then he felt for any other protection spells. There was at least one more. He moved forward a small amount, but did not encounter anything. Luce was slow and cautious as he moved forward once again. He had made it three feet into a nine foot room. For every foot there was another protection spell, through Luce could not feel any beyond the one in front of him and he was running out of energy.

Luce felt around the next protection spell. There was very little he could get back from it. He reached out with his hand and got a shock in return. He withdrew his hand as there was nothing more he could get from the protection spell. This was even more complicated than the last one. Luce went back into the other room. On the floor by the table lay a spell book. He picked it up and flipped through it. Finally he found the spell that was likely used. There was no counter spell listed, but it gave enough information for Luce to figure out what spell could be used. He put the spell book down and went back into the room.

Luce stopped close to the protection barrier. He closed his eyes, shouted out the words, and moved his hands in a horizontal circle instead of a vertical one. When he opened his eyes there were purple sparkles falling as the protection barrier came down. Luce sighed with relief, but felt the tiredness sweep through his body.

Luce reached out to check the next protection spell. There was no shock, or firm wall. It was just a mental idea that he could not push passed. To try and move his hand beyond took too much energy, which he was already low on. If Luce used up anymore he would not have the energy to put the protection spell on the door before he went to bed. As much as Luce wanted to push passed the next protection spell he could not do so until he had rested and gathered more.

Luce sat down on the floor and studied the room. There were no windows. All the light came from one torch on the wall, which had not gone out despite the years that it had been there. The only other thing in the room was the unmade bed. It appeared that the wizard had not bothered to make it before getting himself killed. Most wizards used protection spells on their living spaces as a habit to keep themselves and their belongings safe, but this was the first wizard Luce had encountered who put so many protections spells up. It was strange, unless he was hiding something in this room that he did not want anyone to get their hands on. Whatever the thing is would likely be the one thing which would be the most helpful out of the whole room.

Luce got to his feet. Leaving the room, he closed the door. Luce looked over the stuff in the wizard's work room, but what was not broken was useless to anyone. None of it held any magic. Any of the spell components might be useful if given to another wizard. Luce never bothered with spells that required physical components. He checked over everything again to make sure there was nothing dangerous around for someone else to trip over. There was nothing.

Luce left the tower room and stepped out into outer area of the tower. Sandra was still sitting on the window sill. Luce leaned against next to her. He felt like the stairs were too much work at the moment.

"Did you find anything?" Sandra asked.

"Yes and no," Luce answered, "The bedroom has enough protection spells that there must be something useful to me. However, after three spells to try and get rid of the protection I am too tired to try anymore."

"Well, if we leave now we should get back to the room in time for supper," Sandra said.

"Right," Luce straightened up, but still felt like resting. He opened his cloak and Sandra got into the pocket. Luce started down the stairs. This time it was much harder going. It took all the endurance he could muster to keep going, which meant it took longer to get to the bottom. But he did reach it. He breathing hard and sweating when he reached the bottom, so much so he stopped to rest on the bottom step. He would have mediated for a few minutes in hope of gaining some energy, but he knew the main place he would get the energy was Sandra and it might kill her.

Luce pulled out a handkerchief and wiped his brow. He put it away and took some deep breaths. Finally he got his breath back. He was going to give it a few more minutes before moving when the door to King Driscoll's office opened. Out stepped Rana and the castle steward. The castle steward was off the moment the door closed, but Rana moved slower.

Luce suddenly found slightly more energy than he had the previous moment. He got up and stepped out into the hallway. Rana most have heard him because she turned back.

"Where were you?" Rana asked.

"King Driscoll asked me to check for anything dangerous in the tower room," Luce answered, "He thought I could identify anything and take care of it."

"Is there anything dangerous up there?" Rana asked as they continued along the hallway.

"Not that I have identified so far," Luce answered, "But I have not gotten all the protection spells off the bedroom to check it thoroughly, so it will take me a little longer."

"Well, do not take too long," Rana said, "King Driscoll is making sure the preparations only take two days, so you can leave as soon as possible."

"Hopefully only one more day of working on it," Luce said, "I guess King Driscoll has you helping to make sure everything is ready for when he departs."

"As much as anyone else who is close to him," Rana said, "My brother, Weldon, has his share. The castle steward has more to do than can be done in the amount of time given. However, he will have it done in plenty of time because that is what he does. I have a quarter of the jobs he does and I will barely get them done in time."

"I guess he has to be efficient otherwise he would not have that job," Luce said, "I have never really thought about how much a castle steward does until now."

"Did you grow up in a castle?" Rana asked.

"No, but I have spent some years in one," Luce answered, "I was ambassador of Wodend for ten years. During that time I lived in several castles, but I have never really thought about the servants in them. They seem to blend so well it is difficult to see them if one is not looking specifically for them."

"True," Rana said, "In the last several years, I have done that. It was then that I found out the truth of my birth and parentage. Things like that have a tendency to change a person's viewpoint on much of life."

"I can understand that," Luce said, "I had a sister, who was not my father's child. She died from illness before it was discovered that my mother had an affair."

"At least she did not suffer the indignities of some who were unfortunate to be born in such circumstance," Rana said, "There are some in court who believe that my brother and I should be thrown out of the castle and left to fend for ourselves. King Driscoll scorns all such comments, but that does not stop them."

"It is impossible to get people not to say such things," Luce said, "But they are much easier to ignore if there is someone of power willing to speak up for you."

"True," Rana said with a smile, "What was your sister like?"

"Similar to me in hair colour, eye colour, and skin," Luce answered, "She was a beautiful person on the inside and outside. She was cheerful and could make anyone laugh. She never took anyone for granted and could always find a person's good qualities no matter how cruel they were to her."

"She sounds like a really good person," Rana said, "What happened that her parentage was questioned?"

"There had been plenty of rumours around about my mother's affair, but my father ignored them," Luce said, "It was not brought up until a young gentleman asked for her hand in marriage. No one would have upset things then, but his cousin was highly jealous of him finding happiness. The cousin dug up the affair and the likelihood that my sister was a product of such. This made the gentleman's parents try to pressure him into backing out of the marriage and word getting spread about the whole situation. If she had not fallen ill, everything would have gotten worse. Instead her health disappeared practically overnight, but she survived for a month. The young gentleman visited her every day, but they could not marry while she was sick because the priest refused them that request. When she died all the rumours about the affair died."

"What about your parents?" Rana asked, "What happened with them?"

"My father refused to acknowledge the affair," Luce answered, "He claimed that paying attention to such gossip desecrated the memory of my sister. I have chosen it as she was my sister and the world lost a wonderful person when she died."

"Your father is a wise man," Rana said.

"He was," Luce said.

"What happened?" Rana asked.

"They were in Wodend when it was taken over," Luce answered.

"What do you do now that you have lost you family and your home?" Rana asked.

"I wander from kingdom to kingdom searching for the answer to my own personal quest," Luce answered, "There is not much else to do."

"You have not found someplace to live?" Rana asked.

"No one is willing to take in a refugee from Wodend nobility," Luce answered.

"My mother was from Menano," Rana said, "Driscoll married my mother to prevent the same take over happening to Proster. It was later he found out there is insanity in the royal line. Many people claim the insanity is the reason for the takeover. I am not sure power hungry is the same thing as insanity."

"They look similar," Luce answered, "So some people mistake the two of them. It is experience with both that teaches the difference between the two of them."

"I suppose you have traveled enough to see both of them," Rana said.

"And more," Luce said. They had started up the stairs and he fought to keep up with her and not have his knees buckle.

"I watched my mother go insane," Rana said, "I think that is all I need to see of it."

"Very much," Luce said.

"Do you know how long this trip is going to take?"

Rana asked, "King Driscoll did not seem to know."

"I am not sure," Luce answered.

"Well, Hillel will be glad for a chance to rule," Rana said, "Even if it is for a short time. I suppose he needs the practice. I am just not sure he is ready for it."

"Why is that?" Luce asked.

"Because he has not realized that being king means he has a responsibility to the people of the kingdom," Rana answered, "He still believes it means having the ultimate power and no one to question him. I guess he is power hungry to my mother's insanity."

"Experience," Luce said, "It makes us wonder what we did to deserve this.'

"Yes, that is true," Rana said, "But Driscoll has assigned Weldon and myself to be advisors to Hillel while he is gone. We have to convince him to behave, though he is not likely to do too much because he knows his father will come back and lecture him on his choices. The only thing I am glad about is there are several trustworthy nobles who have volunteered to deal with the lower court, so Weldon's full attention can be directed toward keeping Hillel in line. My word is practically meaningless to Hillel, but I will still do what King Driscoll asks of me."

They reached the top of the stairs and Luce tried to keep the fact that he was out of breath to himself.

"I owe King Driscoll for everything he has done," Rana continued, "And I cannot say no now, even if I know I will not do any good."

"I am sure that King Driscoll would not give you a job if you would not have any effect at all," Luce said. Rana gave him a sad smile.

"Hillel acts differently when his father is around

than when he knows his father will not find out what he is doing," Rana said, "He acts like he is listen to his father when his father is there, but the second King Driscoll leaves the room Hillel turns into a power hungry man. But he stops short of doing things that could be reported to King Driscoll."

"I am sure you will find some way of helping King Driscoll see who his son really is," Luce said.

"I guess I can try," Rana said, "He has put a lot a faith in me."

Luce smiled and Rana smiled back.

"I have to go the library," Rana said, "But I am glad we had this conversation."

"I am glad too," Luce said, "Perhaps we can have another one before I have to leave."

"I hope so," Rana replied. She headed toward the library. Luce waited until she was out of sight before putting a hand on the wall to prevent himself from collapsing. He gave himself a few minutes to rest before moving toward the suite of rooms.

Luce arrived at the same time as the servant with the supper tray. Luce entered first and then stepped out of the way. The servant placed the new tray on the table and took away the old one. Luce closed the door bend the servant. He then turned to the room before opening his cloak. Sandra slipped out of the pocket, shook herself off, and flew to the table. Luce sat down in the chair. They started to eat.

"I will stay here tomorrow," Sandra said, "Then you can take down the protection spells on your own as well as if you want to actually flirt with Rana."

"If I was going to flirt with Rana, I would not worry about whether you were in my pocket or not," Luce said, "But since all I am doing is working in the wizard's rooms, there will not be anything you are needed for. And you don't have to spend more time in my pocket."

"That is the other reason to stay here tomorrow," Sandra said.

"If you do not have enough energy by the time we are ready to leave you will have to ride in my pocket as far as the city gate," Luce said.

"I will work on that," Sandra said. The conversation ended at that and they finished eating without talking. When they were finished, Luce put the protection spell on the door before they went to their rooms for the night.

Luce sat down on the bed and started to mediate to draw power to him. After a couple hours, his head fell to his chest and he was asleep.

After breakfast the next morning, Luce went back up to the tower. No one had been up there since he had left yesterday, but since he had not reported his finding to Driscoll, he had not expected anyone to come clean out the space.

Luce entered the bedroom and got as close to the protection spell as he could. He brought a counter spell to mind. Luce spoke it out loud as he pushed through the barrier with his left hand. There was a bright flash, a loud bang, and the spell was gone. Luce blinked a couple times and shook his head to deal with the effects of the light and the ringing in his ears. Neither seemed to go away so he stepped out of the rom. Both stopped as he passed over the threshold.

Luce enjoyed the quiet as he prepared another

counter spell. Only once he had it ready did Luce step back into the room. The lights and ringing in his ears came back. His mind was confused, but he managed to stutter out the spell he had prepared. The lights and ringing disappeared letting his mind clear. Luce sighed with relief before focusing on the next protection spell.

The spell was not a barrier as much as mental block. Luce found that despite his clear mind he could not remember any spells. He stepped back out of the room and once again the effects were gone. Luce took a piece of parchment along with quill and ink. He checked to make sure none of them had magical qualities, which they did not. Then he wrote the counter spell on the piece of parchment.

Luce took the parchment into the room and found the spell leave his head. He looked down at the piece of parchment. The words appeared to be nonsense. Luce read them out loud anyway. The piece of parchment burned up as the spell worked. There was a fireworks display of purples, pinks, blues, and greens. Luce closed his eyes to it all, but he could still see the flashes until they slowly faded away. Once the lights were gone, Luce opened his eyes. There was a burned circle on the floor, but otherwise the protection spell was gone.

Luce felt like all his energy had vanished and he staggered into the other room. He collapsed on the floor on the other side of the threshold. Luce managed to pull himself up against the wall. He closed his eyes and started to draw energy from everything around him. The skeleton of the wizard had some energy left from whatever spells he had prepared but had not used.

When the skeleton was drained, Luce kept looking

for energy. Some of the spell components had small amounts of energy. A few of the other objects were similar. But there was something else in the room with a lot of energy. Whatever it was Luce was not able to sense it except through looking for where the energy source was. He did not drain the energy from whatever it, but instead tried to figure where it was in the room. It appeared to be under some rubble in the corner where a shelf had fallen down.

Luce came back to himself. He was careful as he got up. Going from little energy to lots of energy tended to make him unstable. The first few steps tottering, but slowly got better. He was steady by the time he reached the corner. Luce moved the debris until he uncovered a cage. Lying in the bottom of the cage was a silver dragon the length of Luce's hand. It was likely being raised as a familiar for the wizard before the wizard died. Now the dragon was barely alive, though still was creating its own energy.

The dragon did not move when Luce opened the cage. He put his hand near the dragon's nose. The dragon sniffed at it without moving. It stuck its tongue out far enough to lick Luce's finger, but just withdrew its tongue. Luce closed the cage. He left the dragon and headed for the stairs, which were easy because of the amount of energy he currently had. There was no one in the hallway at the bottom. Luce headed for the kitchen. Everyone there was busy working on lunch. Luce got some bread, meat, and water without being noticed. He took them and went back to the stairs to the tower.

When Luce turned down the hallway to the stairs, Rana turned down the hallway coming from the other direction.

"Good morning," Rana smiled.

"Good morning to you," Luce responded with a smile of his own.

"You look like you are doing better today," Rana said, "You are almost glowing."

"I likely am glowing," Luce said, "I have been absorbing energy to deal with the protection spells in the tower. It tends to make a person appear as if they radiating light."

"And the early lunch?" Rana asked.

"It is not for me," Luce answered, "I found someone who needs a good meal."

"There is someone else up in the tower?" Rana asked.

"Sort of," Luce answered, "It is a dragon."

"And it survived being up there by itself?" Rana asked.

"Dragons are actually hardy beasts," Luce answered, "They can last a long time without food or water because they survive on what energy they can create within themselves. However, eventually they use themselves up. This one is close to death, but with some food and care it will survive."

"May I come up and see it?" Rana asked.

"Sure," Luce answered. They reached the bottom of the stairs. Luce let Rana go up ahead of him. She was panting by the time they reached the top. Rana looked at him and the fact he was not even breathing heavy.

"Endurance from all the time I have spent wandering to world," Luce answered to her look.

"I have spent too much time stuck in the palace," Rana said. Luce led the way into the tower room. Rana followed at a slower pace as she took the room in. Luce picked up the dragon's cage and brought it out to the middle of the room where there was more space. Rana stopped and stared at the skeleton.

"What happened to his head?" Rana asked.

"My guess is that it was stolen," Luce answered, "But when and by who, I do not know."

"Why would anyone want the head of a wizard?" Rana asked as she sat down by beside the cage.

"The skull sells for a good chunk of money," Luce suggested as he sat down.

"It looks so cute," Rana said looking at the dragon.

"Right now it does not have the energy to be dangerous," Luce said, "But once it has some food in it, that might change." Luce unlocked the cage.

"Can I give it the first piece?" Rana asked.

"Sure," Luce answered holding out the plate. Rana took a small piece of the meat before sticking her hand in the cage. She held the meat near the dragon's nose. It sniffed and then stuck out its tongue. It licked the meat and gave a small smile. The dragon withdrew its tongue, but left its mouth open. Rana placed the meat in the dragon's mouth and then removed her fingers before the dragon closed its mouth.

"How do you tell if a dragon is male or female?" Rana asked.

"You ask it," Luce answered, "Once this one had perked up a bit you might be able to ask it and get an answer, but it will take a little bit before it will have the strength to answer."

The dragon chewed on the meat for a few minutes and then swallowed. It sat for a few minutes and then made a squealing sound.

"What does that mean?" Rana asked.

"It is still hungry," Luce said as he tore off a piece of the bread. He held it in front of the dragon's mouth. The dragon opened its mouth and Luce placed the bread inside. The dragon closed its mouth, chewed, and then swallowed. It licked its lips and opened its mouth for more, which Rana picked off the plate and fed to it.

Luce and Rana took turns feeding the dragon until they ran out of food. When it was done the dragon lifted its head and looked at them as if it was asking for more. Rana smiled at it.

"I will go get you some more," Rana said, "You just have to give me a few minutes." The dragon seemed to sigh and then rested its head back down.

"It likes you," Luce said.

"I better go," Rana said. She smiled at Luce as she got to her feet.

"I should get back to the protection spells," Luce said, "If the dragon does not mind sitting alone." The dragon seemed to shrug.

"Might be more energetic after some food," Rana said. She left the room.

"Male or female?" Luce asked the dragon. The dragon puffed out its chest and breathed out a cold breath that left ice crystals on the bar of the cage.

"Male then," Luce said. The dragon gave him a look that said of course.

"Okay," Luce said, "I am going off now." Luce got to his feet and went into the bedroom.

Luce walked around the barrier, which he could feel with his hand without getting injured. The barrier went around the bed, but that was all it covered. Luce examined it as much as he could. He thought up a counter spell. Once it was firm in his mind, Luce started to say it out loud. Before he could finish it, Luce realized that the spell was warping his words and stopped. The energy hung in the air. Luce sat down on the floor cross legged and closed his eyes. He worked to absorb the energy from the spell back into himself. As he did so, Luce found that he was getting energy from the barrier. So, he just started absorbing as much of the energy as he could from the protection barrier.

Luce hit the point where he usually stopped for fear of getting too much and having it destroy his mind. But there was still some energy left in the barrier. Luce thought about quitting, or going off to get rid of some of the energy, but instead he kept at it.

Finally the energy was gone. Luce felt like he had so much power he could take on anything and everything. There was a little voice in the back of his head that suggested all these thoughts were bad things, but there was so much power running through his body it could not be a bad thing. He started to get to his feet, but found a magical barrier in front of him. No magical barrier was going to stop him from getting anywhere, or doing whatever he wanted to do. Luce poured his energy into this new barrier in an effort to get rid of it.

The barrier absorbed much of the energy, but eventually became over powered by the amount of energy. It dissolved into a shower of blue sparkles. Luce had a lot less energy now and his thoughts were no longer on the power to conquer the world. He shook his head to clear away any lingering effects of the power. Then he focused on the next protection spell, but could not find another one. Luce sighed and stepped closer to the bed. He did not encounter any other spells. Luce laid both hands on the bed and searched for anything else that may be magical, but found nothing there.

Luce sat back down with his back to the wall and stared at the bed. He knew that many wizards were highly paranoid about their sleeping place to put many protection spells up, but never to the extent that he had brought down from this room and this bed. No one was that paranoid, were they? Luce leaned his head back in frustration.

There was a skittering sound, like claws on stone floor. Luce looked and saw the dragon cross from the door to the bed. Rana stepped into the doorway.

"Where is he going?" Luce asked as he got to his feet.

"I do not know," Rana answered, "He had climbed out of the cage when I got back with the food, but he stayed there until just a moment ago when he headed in here."

The dragon had climbed up on the bed and Luce could see him moving around the bedding.

"Well, unless he is planning to make nest he should not be in there," Luce said. He reached out and pulled some of the bedding back trying to find the dragon. The dragon was too fast and had already moved, so Luce pulled the blanket right off the bed. The dragon has somehow managed to get under the top sheet. Luce pulled this off the bed as well. The dragon did not go with it, but was under the bottom sheet.

"He is fast," Rana said.

"Yes, he is," Luce said as he pulled out the bottom sheet and yanked it off the bed. The dragon stayed on the bed by digging in his claws. Luce's attention was drawn from the dragon to a hole in the mattress that was about a foot in length and width. In the centre was a wooden box which took up all the space so that the mattress might as well have been flat. The dragon growled at the box and did not move closer to it.

"And that would be a good reason for all the protection spells," Luce said as he gently picked up the dragon. He offered the dragon to Rana who held out her hand. Luce placed it in her palm and it curled up as if it found a comfortable place to sleep.

"Why did he not like the box?" Rana asked.

"Likely another protection is on it," Luce answered, "It feels wrong to him and I do not feel it at all. The best thing to do is to figure out what is on the box before touching it. There are some very powerful ways to protect things without actually using a spell. Best to take him out of here. I will have to think about this problem for a while and then do some experiments."

"Perhaps you should stop and eat lunch before you start experimenting," Rana said, "You look worn out."

"A break is a good idea," Luce said. They left the bedroom and went out to the other room.

"What should we do with this little guy?" Rana asked petted the dragon's head. The dragon yawned and snuggled into Rana's hand. Luce and Rana started toward the stairs.

"I would say that he is very comfortable with you," Luce said, "Perhaps you would like a pet." The dragon had fallen asleep as they headed down the stairs.

"But what do I do when he gets bigger?" Rana asked.

"He may not get bigger," Luce answered, "The wizard wanted him as a familiar and having a large dragon as a familiar is not a good idea. This dragon could be a breed which does not get very big. I would suggest taking him back to the portal where his kind is from, but I do not think he will going willingly."

"I guess having a dragon as a pet might be a good thing," Rana said, "He would be great protection. If anyone tries to hurt me he can just breathe fire and drive them away."

"He is a silver dragon," Luce said, "He does not breathe fire, but has ice as his breath weapon. So, he can freeze people for you instead of setting them on fire."

"Same result," Rana said.

"True," Luce replied.

"I just need to find someplace to keep him," Rana said, "I cannot keep him with me at all times. It is best if a very limited number of people know I have him.'

"Probably a good idea," Luce said, "Some people have problems with creatures that have magical properties. Or are seen as not naturally residing in the world."

"There are also a few who would wish to take him for themselves," Rana said, "Driscoll loves creatures not of this world and spends much of his time reading about them or researching them."

"I have seen it," Luce said, "I have a fairy with me because we are both searching for the same thing. When I first talked to him, Driscoll saw her and looked like he wanted to know everything about her. Yesterday he promised that even if we find what we are looking for he would return here."

"He will keep his promise," Rana said, "But he will wish for the opposite."

"I am only concerned that he keeps his promise,"

Luce said, "Anything else that goes through his head does not matter as much to me as his actions."

"So, what are you looking for, that a fairy would also be looking for?" Rana asked.

"There is a portal in this part of the world through which magic used to come," Luce answered, "But some time ago the magic disappeared. So, my quest has been to figure out what happened and I believe the portal had something to do with it."

"Will you come back from your quest?" Rana asked.

"I do not know," Luce answered, "The guardian may feel I am not worthy to cross over. Or there may be a more simple explanation which does not involve me leaving this world. I am not looking to leave this world, but merely figure out what happened to the magic."

"I see," Rana said, "And if you were offered a chance to live there?"

"I do not know," Luce answered, "I have no home here, but would it be any different in a world where humans are the minority and usually considered trouble. It may be better to stay in this world because I know my enemies and how to avoid them. There is a lot to think about before I could make that kind of decision."

Rana nodded. They reached the bottom of the stairs and found the hallway empty.

"I should take the dragon to my room before going to the dining room," Rana said.

"I will be eating in my room," Luce said, "I find most people are more comfortable with that."

"Then perhaps we will talk again," Rana said.

"I hope so," Luce said. They smiled at each other and then Rana hurried off before someone came. She went fast enough that after the first turn, Luce did not see her. He went up to his room, where the servant had just finished delivering the lunch tray.

After lunch was finished, Luce headed back up to the tower. He had reached the hallway when he met up with Driscoll, who was headed back to his office having just finished eating.

"Good afternoon," Driscoll said.

"Good afternoon, you majesty," Luce answered.

"Have you found anything in the tower?" Driscoll asked.

"I may have," Luce answered, "Most of the stuff in the tower is useless and has no magic. Things like spell components, where they are harmless until put into the spell. I do not use any spells involving components, so they are meaningless to me. The wizard's skeleton is still up there, but someone broke in and stole to skull most likely to sell it."

"Why would anyone want a skull?" Driscoll asked.

"Belief in its magical properties, I think," Luce answered, "It does not have any actual magical properties, but that does not stop people from believing."

"But the skull was not what you think you found," Driscoll said.

"No," Luce said, "I took down the protection spells from the bedroom and found a box in the bed which may contain something worthwhile. I will not know exactly what it is until I figure out how to open it."

"When I can send someone up to clean out the rooms?" Driscoll asked.

"Late this afternoon," Luce answered, "I am finished with the outer room, but I would prefer not to have anyone up there while I try and figure out how to get in the box." They reached the door to Driscoll's study, but he did not open it.

"Understandable," Driscoll said, "Are you ready to leave tomorrow morning?"

"Yes," Luce answered.

"I expect you do not have a horse of your own," Driscoll said.

"That would be correct," Luce replied.

"Then you will be supplied with one from the royal stables," Driscoll said, "It will speed up the journey to the forest."

"I appreciate that," Luce said with a slight bow.

"You are welcome," Driscoll said.

"If you would excuse me," Luce said.

"You are excused," Driscoll said. Luce headed for the stairs while Driscoll went into his office.

At the top of the stairs, Luce went directly into the bedroom. He studied the box for several minutes. He left the room and went into outer room. He picked up a long stick, which gave off no indication of magic, and took it back into the bedroom. Luce used the tick to touch the box. The stick burst into flames on contact. Luce put it out quickly. He went back to the outer room. He left the stick where he had found it.

Luce looked through the debris. He found a roll of parchment and took it back into the bedroom. This time the parchment just turned to dust and Luce had to drop it before it reached his hand. He went back out and searched through the debris again. There was very little that was the right length and sturdy to use. Finally he picked up the wizard's staff. There was no more magic in the staff and the crystal was broken. It was now just a walking stick.

Luce took it into the bedroom and touched it to the box. It did not light on fire, or turn to dust. Luce used it to leaver the box out of the mattress with a large amount of difficulty. It came out and rolled off the bed on the other side. Luce went around the bed. The box had landed with the top up and he sighed with relief. He used the staff to pop the latch and open the lid.

Inside the box was a silver amulet on a silver chain. The amulet had been engraved with the symbol of the Saint Onan, who was the saint of power. Luce put the staff through the chain and lifted the amulet out of the box. The chain slide down the staff and Luce caught it. The chain gave off power, but it was not protected. Holding it, Luce could feel it was a powerful item. He placed it around his neck. His energy level topped up, but did not go over the level he was comfortable with. Luce slipped the amulet under his shirt before turning his attention back to the box.

He used the staff to close the lid. Then he went back out to the other room. He picked up the charred stick and took it with him back into the bedroom. He dropped it on top of the box. The stick burst into flames. In a minute the box was also in fire. Luce sat down on the floor and watched the box burn. Once the box and stick were consumed the fire ran out of fuel and died out. Luce spread the ashes out on the stone floor and then watched for a few more seconds to make sure it was out. Then Luce left the bedroom for the last time.

He headed down the stairs and did not meet anyone in the hallway leading to the stairs. Once he was in the main hallway, no one paid much attention to him and he was able to get back to the suite without being interrupted. Inside the suite, Luce found Sandra sitting in the chair reading a book that matched her in size. She looked up at him when he closed the door. She looked at him for a long moment without saying anything.

"Where did you find so much energy?" Sandra asked.

"This," Luce answered pulling out the amulet. He removed it from his neck and held it for her to see.

"You found an amulet of Saint Onan?" Sandra asked.

"It was what was hidden in the wizard's tower," Luce answered. He set the amulet on the chair in front of Sandra. She set the book aside to pick up the amulet.

"There are only three of these," Sandra said, "And they are the most powerful magical objects ever made." She started to glow brighter.

"And this is what is going to give us energy until we find the portal," Luce said, "And it may be the source of energy for me for the rest of my life if I do not figure out what happened to the magic around here."

"I feel so much better now," Sandra said, "I will definitely be able to use my invisibility tomorrow."

"Good," Luce said, "I will leave it here with you. I am done in the tower now, so I am going to spend the rest of today in the library with my favourite book from the last time I was here."

"Enjoy," Sandra said as she set down the amulet. She was bright enough she could be her own light source and Luce could not look directly at her. He could not tell if she had gone back to her book or was looking at him. He left the room and headed for the library.

The library was empty when he entered. Luce found the book quickly because it was exactly where he remembered it being. He took it and went to the chair in the far corner to read. There was barely enough light to read by from the windows, but that was okay with him.

The sound of books being dropped caused Luce to raise his head off his chest, where it had fallen when he had lost the fight with the urge to nap. He was still as he waited for the next sound. It came fairly quickly after the first one. There was the sound of claws on floor and the shuffling of books. It sounded like the person was picking up the books.

"I told you to stay still," Rana's voice came from the shelves, "If you cannot stay still, I will have to either keep you in a pocket or leave you in the room." There was a squeal and then the sound of hurried clicking.

The dragon came out from the shelves and came over to Luce. He used his wings to jump up on the arm rest of the chair. He rubbed the top of his head against Luce's wrist until Luce scratched him.

"Now, where did you go?" It sounded like Rana had finished picking up the books before looking for the dragon. She came out of the shelves where the dragon had. She looked surprised to see Luce.

"Finished with the box in the tower?" Rana asked.

"Yes," Luce answered, "It had a powerful amulet in it. I left it in my suite before coming here to spend the afternoon with my favourite book." Luce held up the book with his free hand. Rana studied the cover for a moment.

"The Prince and the Rogue," Rana read, "I do not think I have read that one."

"It is a very good book," Luce said, "You should read it some time."

"Perhaps when I finish the ones I have," Rana said indicating the six thick volumes she had in her arms, "The dragon does not seem to want to stay in my room."

"He is attached to you," Luce said, "I believe it is a common thing when they decide they really like you."

"Then I am going to have sew a special pocket for him into all of my clothes," Rana said, "Because that will be the only way to protect him."

"I am sure that he will understand if you explain it to him," Luce said, "As long as you do not try to leave him behind."

"I will try that," Rana said.

"Have you named him yet?" Luce asked.

"No," Rana answered, "But I am sure the right name will come to me eventually.'

"I am sure it will," Luce said. Rana smiled before holding her hand out. The dragon thought about it, looked at Luce who quit scratching his head, and then shrugged to itself before going across to Rana's hand. He curled up and got comfortable.

"Thank you," Rana said.

"You are welcome," Luce replied. Rana headed for the library door. Luce watched her go before trying to go back to his book.

Eventually Luce gave up and went back to his suite where the lunch tray had been exchanged for the supper tray. After supper, Luce headed for bed.

THEY LEAVE ON THEIR JOURNEY AND ENTER THE ENCHANTED FOREST

The sun had not yet come over the horizon when Luce had finished packing his belongings. Or repacking was mostly what he was doing. He had not unpacked much and all he had to add was the amulet, which he wore under his shirt. His cloak held most of his belongings and aside from shifting things from one pocket to another he never unpacked any of it.

Sandra was also up and ready. If she had a pack, Luce had never seen it. However, there were occasions when she had things she could have only brought with her. Luce never asked about any of it, but left her alone.

They had not been brought up breakfast, but no one had come and gotten the supper tray either. Since they were both ready to go, Luce decided he did not need to wait for them to bring the food up. He checked that they had everything. Sandra turned herself invisible and settled on his shoulder. Then Luce picked up the tray and left the suite.

In the kitchen everyone was working on making breakfast. However, someone took the time to take the tray and provide a small amount to eat. Luce accepted it and left the kitchen. He gave some to Sandra and ate the rest as he headed for Driscoll's office. Luce knocked on the door, but there was no answer. He opened the door and looked in. There were no lights on and no one inside.

Luce headed for the stables. He did not meet anyone on the way, but found the stable master was having the stable hands get five horses ready. Luce wandered out into the courtyard where everything was quiet and found a place to sit. He sat there and leaned against the wall as he watched the sky lighten. It was chilly out with the coming of winter, but otherwise was a nice beginning to a day.

The sun was just about over the castle wall before others came out of the stable. The first to come out were two uniformed guards. Then there was a nobleman who Luce had seen before, but did not know the name of. A stable hand was next, but he was leading the horse, not riding it. Luce stood up and accepted the reins. Finally King Driscoll came out leading his horse. He was wearing clothing appropriate for traveling and adventuring, unlike the nobleman who was wearing whatever he would wear on a regular day with a warm cloak over top.

"There are a few people who wanted to say good bye to us before we leave," Driscoll said as he walked passed Luce, "They are by the front door."

Luce followed Driscoll while leading his horse. They came around and found standing beside the door were three people. Rana was there along with a man who looked similar and Luce assumed was Weldon, her brother. The third was a woman who wore expensive clothes, had long brown hair braided back, and the face of someone who had spent a large part of their life working in a field. Luce did not remember seeing her around, but he had not been paying attention this trip.

"Good luck," Weldon said as he shook Driscoll's hand.

"Watch over him until I get back," Driscoll said.

"We will," Weldon said.

"Come back safe," Rana said before giving Driscoll a hug.

"I will try my best," Driscoll said. Weldon stepped back and Rana went towards Luce.

"I named him Eustace," Rana said to Luce.

"Good name," Luce said. They exchanged smiled and she stepped back to stand next to Weldon. The other woman had stepped up to Driscoll and whispered in his ear. If he whispered anything back Luce could not tell. Driscoll instead kissed her on the forehead. She hugged him briefly and then stepped back.

Luce and Driscoll mounted their horses and then led the way out of the courtyard gates. The other three followed.

"I understand the guards," Luce spoke in a low volume, "But who is the nobleman?"

"Lord Salisbury refused to let me leave without him," Driscoll spoke in the same volume, "He has been my advisor for many years and tried to advise against me going at all. When I told I was going anyway, he decided he must come along. He will be some trouble, but hopefully not much. I tried to tell him certain things about adventuring. As you can see by his outfit, he did not listen."

"As long as he stays out of the way," Luce said.

"He will," Driscoll replied.

They did not speak as they rode through the streets of the city on their way down to the gate. The people of the city were starting their day. So they were out and about, but wearing warmer clothing to keep off the chill. They barely glanced up at the group as it passed. The people had no concern about some riders going off on an adventure which did not affect them and none recognized the king.

Once the group reached the city gates they turned left and went along the road. They continued along it until they reached the end of the city wall at which point they turned left off the road. They followed the strip of grassy area between the city wall and the forest for a while.

"Did you remarry after your wife died?" Luce asked Driscoll.

"No," Driscoll answered, "I could not think to do such a thing. She may have suffered, but there are few in the court who would consider my remarrying a desecration of her memory. Not that I have had any problems. Her memory is not something I choose to commemorate."

"Who was the lady back at the castle then?" Luce asked.

"That is Malise," Driscoll answered, "She started out

her life as the daughter of a chambermaid and grew up to be a chambermaid herself. I fell in love with her before either of us truly understood what love was and how it would affect our lives. She is the mother of Hillel, but he will never know that."

"What happened?" Luce asked.

"She helped me deal with my father's death," Driscoll said, "But shortly after we found she was with child and I knew she could not stay at court without there being a scandal. So, I send her off to the country estate where she gave birth to Hillel. She raised him to the age of about three before she gave him over to a governess. Then she went off and found a job working in someone's field. I went out to visit the estate about three times a year, at least one of them around his birthday. I was saddened by her departure, but it had been her choice.

"And then the army took over Wodend without us having enough notice to help at all. They sent an offer of peace here to Proster and I could not turn them down. The agreement was that I marry their princess and they would not try and take over Proster. So, I married their princess who had her guard as her lover and he left his own children within her. It was not much of a marriage, but Weldon and Rana turned out all right. On my fortieth birthday, I announced my heir, which of course is my first born. So, I went back out to the country estate and brought him and his wife back. While I was out there, I found Malise again when I passed the field and saw her working. I begged her to come back with me to the castle and be my love once again. She agreed. Since then I have given her everything she needs or wants. The court accepted her to a certain extent, probably because they know I would be highly upset if they did not. So, that woman was Malise."

"I see," Luce said.

"Have you got a wife somewhere?" Driscoll asked.

"No," Luce answered, "My family believed in marrying for love and I never found anyone who I felt I loved."

"Despite its fickle nature, love is a wonderful thing," Driscoll said.

"Your father thought so," Luce said, "He worshiped Saint Lang, the saint of true love. It is more the pity he never found his true love."

"He loved my mother for much," Driscoll said, "Even after her death he never found another, even for company."

"He loved your mother because of you," Luce said, "And it was enough for him because he knew how fragile love could be. He understood that the world can destroy everything in one moment in time."

"You do not believe my mother was his true love," Driscoll said looking at Luce in surprise.

"I know it was not," Luce answered, "He had found his true love, but he could not find the courage to talk to her. Then she was gone before he found it, so he went with the next best thing at the promise of children he could love."

"But he did find love," Driscoll said.

"Most humans do," Luce replied, "It is you with your dwarf blood that feel there is only one love. Though friendship can turn to love or look like it to an outside person. It is more about appearances than truth."

"I suppose that is good enough," Driscoll said, "Though I would wish more for him."

Before Luce could respond, the horse of one of the guards tripped up and just about tossed the guard. He only barely managed to hold on and then calm the horse down. Everyone stopped. When the horse was calm enough, the guard got down and did an examination.

"He lost a shoe," the guard said, "He cannot go on until it is fixed."

"We are still close to the city," Driscoll responded, "Take him to the farrier and get it fixed. Once you are, you can either wait for it to be fixed, or find another horse for the rest of the journey. We will get as far as the place marked on the map as the entrance to the forest and then we will camp to wait for you."

"Yes, you highness," the guard said with a bow. Then he led his horse back toward the city while the rest of the group moved on. The conversation did not continue as they rode, but instead each man stayed with his own thoughts.

They reached the path going into the forest a little after midday. Everyone helped out to set up camp. Once the camp was up, Luce helped the guard named Tarak to fix lunch. When lunch was over, everyone sat there around the fire and waited for word from the other guard, Wyman.

"Perhaps a story," Lord Salisbury suggested.

"Good idea," Driscoll said, "I think I have a good one. It is a bit contemporary, but it includes the use of magic. Anyway, a group of friends met in a local tavern…"

Well, actually they had received invitations to meet with the local noble lady, who needed their help with something that she felt she could not specify in the letter. As the five travelers were in separate places when they received the letters, they all met up at the tavern in the town.

The dwarf was the first to arrive because he was closest. The dwarf was known as Brian. He was tall for a dwarf at five two, weighed about a hundred and eighty pounds and had the usual broad build. He had tanned skin, blue eyes, brown beard and hair carefully styled. He was known for the colourful tunics that could be seen under the pieces of plate mail, this particular day he wore a bright blue tunic with black trousers and boots. He also wore silver earrings, an ornament in his beard right below his lip, and a gold ring on his right hand. The only weapon he carried was an old axe, which had been given to him by his father, that was said to have magical properties but no one could say what it was. He did not have any other weapons on him because the only ones he used, and used well, were his fists.

Brian was several days early so he found himself a room and spent the time in the tavern drinking. He must have been flush from a previous adventure because he never seemed to run out of money for the next drink.

The next member of the party to arrive was the half-elf named Julie. This half-elf was five feet five inches, a hundred pounds and thin build. She had long brown hair with bangs that ended just above her brown eyes, and pale skin. She wore a red tunic, black leggings, and brown boots. She had silver earrings, a silver medallion, and a gold ring on her left hand. Her weapons were a small dagger and her fife. She was a bard, so she created magic through her music which was what she used to fight with when she had to fight.

It took a day and a half for Julie to get to town. Being a bard, she was welcomed at the tavern. She would spend some of the time playing for the patrons and some time trading stories with Brian.

The next to arrive was the human wizard, who was named Paul. He was five seven with a lean build but not skinny, a hundred and forty-two pounds. He had light skin, short dark hair, and grey eyes. He wore grey robes likely over tunic and trousers as well as grey shoes. The robes looked to be plain by the light of the sun, but in dark places symbols would appear. He had a belt with several pouches hanging off it with everything he needed for his spells. He also had a silver ring on each hand. His weapons were illusions and logic all of which came from either his spell book or his head.

Paul arrived two days after Julie and made himself comfortable in his room, where he would spend most of his days. He would come out in the evening and join the other two in the tavern.

The gnome and her companion arrived next. The gnome was named Sherry. She was three feet tall, forty-two pounds, and solidly built. Her skin was tanned, short spiky black hair, and blue eyes. She wore a black tunic, black leggings, and matching black jacket and *boots with silver buckles. Also she wore several silver rings and a silver bracelet on her right wrist. The gnome was a rogue, whose specialization was in disarming traps and getting through locks.*

Her companion was an elf she had been traveling around with for a couple years now. His name was Todd. He was six feet tall, a hundred fifteen pounds, and slender. His skin was lightly tanned, his hair was long blond, and his eyes were deep brown. His outfit was elven made from the finest weaved elven fabric and was deep green with gold trim. He was a ranger and thus carried with him his bow and arrows over one shoulder as well as a sword at his side with a dagger in his boot.

They arrived a day later than Paul. Sherry spent most her time in the tavern with the dwarf, while Todd wandered the town investigating what he could. He would join the rest in the evenings when they got together to talk.

The last to arrive was the human cleric named Glenda. She was five feet four inches, a hundred forty pounds, and medium build. Her skin was pale from spending too much time out of the sun, white shoulder length hair, and blue eyes. She wore a white animal skin shirt, black animal skin trousers, and pieces of leather armour. Also one gold ring on the left hand and a bracelet also on the left wrist. Her speciality was healing and herbology.

Glenda arrived in the afternoon and spent the rest of the day in the tavern. They were not able to have their usual evening conversation because Julie was to provide the music for the evening, Todd had not come back from his wanderings, and Paul had to spend the time talking with the apprentice he left to take care of things back at his tower. By the time all that was sorted out, it was too late. Glenda took a corner of the room shared by Julie and Sherry. Brian, Paul, and Todd shared a second room.

The next morning, they all gathered in the tavern for breakfast. They sat down at one of the tables, with Todd dragging an extra chair over for himself. The owner brought them all breakfast and then left them alone.

"So, what do we know about this Lady Erica?" Glenda asked.

"Her holding is just south of here," Todd answered, "The people below her see her as kind and think well of her. She is a strong connection with the royal family, but does not spend time at court. Her brother and his wife lived with her before they died. Now her niece lives with her, but no one has seen the niece in a couple weeks. Lady Erica is known to pay her debts and pay well anyone she hires."

"Everyone in town speaks well of her," Brian said, "They invite her to many of their events and she usually shows up. She has not been around for a while because it is a busy time at her holding."

"Should we go see what she needs help with?" Paul asked.

"Sure," Sherry said.

"I believe we should," Glenda said.

"Sounds interesting," Brian said with a shrug.

"Then we shall go hear Lady Erica out," Paul said, "As soon as we finish breakfast."

Everyone nodded.

"Did you find someone to look after your herb garden?" Julie asked.

"Yes," Glenda answered, "I found a girl named Loraine to look after them while I am gone. She is good with the plants and I have had a chance to give her enough training that she knows what to do. Did you get the position you were trying for? The one as the king's player?"

"No," Julie answered, "He did not think the fife was an appropriate instrument for court, but by then I had heard the rumours of war. I got out of the country just in time for the attacks to start. It was all within the country, but that does not make it any less dangerous."

"Best kind," Brian said, "Depending on which side had the most gold."

"Neither," Julie answered, "Just belief in their side being right."

"I see why you did not stay," Brian said.

"Is that what you have been doing?" Sherry asked, "Fighting wars?"

"I have fought in a couple skirmishes," Brian answered, "Enough to pay my tab."

"What rich king did you manage to swindle then?" Sherry asked, "Because you appear to have enough to drink the rest of your life away."

"Well, they have been good paying skirmishes," Brian answered, "What trouble have you been getting into?"

"Not much," Sherry answered, "No wars, but the king of sociology used to advertise that his treasury could not be broken into by any person alive."

"He no longer advertises such a thing?" Brian asked.

"And I gained a pouchful of gold as well," Sherry answered, *"Though I no longer have much left."*

"Spent it?" Brian asked.

"On the journey to the temple of Meslow," Sherry answered.

"Did you meet him?" Glenda asked.

"No, but Todd and I spent time studying the texts there," Sherry answered, *"But hopefully someday he will show himself to us. If this jobs pays enough we will go back there. Have you been back to the temple of Polva, Brian?"*

"No," Brian answered, *"I studied the texts and I had a brief discussion with him, which was fantastic. I learned all I could from studying him, so I moved on to studying other things when I have time. What about you, Paul? What are you studying?"*

"Word puzzles," Paula answered, *"Mostly making them. My apprentice, Ian, has been working with me on it. The magic generated through them is enormous. Every time I run more words through the puzzles I find more to study. It is fascinating."*

"Sounds like it," Brian said, *"Anything we can use on this job?"*

"Maybe a few things," Paul answered, *"Depends on what we end up having to do."*

"Maybe we should get moving," Glenda said.

Everyone looked around and realized they were all finished eating. So they left the money on the table for the food and exited the tavern. They stopped in their rooms to gather their belongings before heading off down the road toward Lady Erica's estate.

It was close to noon when they reached the gates of the house. There was a guard at the gate who stopped them.

"What do you want here?" the guard asked of them.

"We have received an invitation from Lady Erica to come," Glenda answered holding out her copy of the letter. The guard took it and looked it over. Finally he nodded and handed the letter back.

"Go straight up to the door," the guard instructed, "Godfrey will take you in to see Lady Erica."

"Thank you," Glenda said. The guard stepped back out of the way. The group moved on into the court yard which was a cobblestone path that went in a circle around the fountain and passed the steps. The fountain was a maiden pouring water out of a jug standing in the middle of a large basin. There was a row of flowers around the base. The house itself was large and made out of white stone. The entry was two storeys and the building stretched out to have wings on either side.

When the group reached the steps, a man stood there in a black and white suit with a stiff posture. The man looked the group for a moment.

"This way," he finally said. Then he turned and went into the house. The group went up the steps and followed him inside. The decorations inside were expensive, but minimalistic. It was tastefully done. There was a grand staircase straight ahead and a hallway in each direction just behind it. There were two doors, one on each side, closer to the door.

Godfrey led them to the door on the left. He knocked

on the door before opening it. He stepped inside and said something before holding the door open for the group to enter. This room had three walls of shelves with the fourth one being windows. All the shelves were filled with books. There were numerous chairs spread out around the room and a chesterfield in front of the window. At one end of the room was a desk covered with stacks of paper, quills, ink pots, and a couple of books. Behind the desk sat a woman, who the group assumed was Lady Erica. She wore a flattering emerald dress and her brown hair pulled up. Lady Erica wore little jewellery with only a necklace with a charm on it and a silver ring on her right hand. She wore a pair of spectacles which kept slipping down her nose and a worried look on her face.

Lady Erica rose to greet them. She smiled, but her orbicularis oculi muscle did not engage.

"Welcome," Lady Erica said, "Have a seat."

Everyone in the group found a chair to sit in. A few had to drag one over. Once they were sitting down, Lady Erica also sat down. Godfrey left the room.

"Thank you for coming so promptly," Lady Erica said, "I asked you here because I really need your help to find my niece, Dawn. She is twelve years old."

"What happened?" Glenda asked.

"She went out with the stable master for a riding lesson," Lady Erica answered, "He came back two hours later and barely made it. He said they had been attacked by a group of goblins with the help of a stone creature. Dawn had been taken away by the stone creature and once the stable master was unconscious the goblins must have followed it. The stone creature

and the goblins left a trail that was easy to follow across the field and into the forest. Unfortunately there is none among my staff who was willing to go into the forest.

"I heard of you through one of my workers. You helped the village his brother lives in from the werewolves. I was hoping that you would be willing to help search for my niece."

The group looked at each other and each nodded in turn.

"We will try our best to see if we can find your niece," Glenda said.

"Thank you," Lady Erica said."

Luce heard the sound of hoof beats and Driscoll stopped the story. They all looked up to see the guard, Wyman, coming toward them. Tarak went to greet his fellow guard. Luce paid attention to the rest of the area. The sun was sinking behind the trees and the day time animals were disappearing for the night.

Wyman and Tarak got back to camp. Wyman tied up his horse and then joined Tarak in making supper. Luce did what he could to help. Driscoll and Lord Salisbury talked to each other. Finally supper was finished and everyone was given a plate.

By the time they were finished eating it was dark. Luce volunteered to clean up. He quickly dealt with all the dishes. Then everyone climbed into their bedroll for the night.

Luce woke to find the sky was still dark. He lay there for several minutes trying to figure out what woke him. All he heard was the regular night sounds. Luce rolled over on to his side preparing to go back to sleep. He froze at the sight of Sandra standing there with her hands on her hips and glaring at him.

"What did I do?" Luce whispered.

"It is time to get up and moving," Sandra snapped in a whisper.

Luce looked up at the sky and saw the stars had moved to their positions which meant there was another hour until the sun would come up.

"It is the middle of the night," Luce whispered back.

"Humans," Sandra sighed, "Can you not feel that?"

Luce reached out with his senses, but he could not sense anything out of the ordinary. He shook his head.

"I do not sense anything," Luce answered.

"Then trust," Sandra said, "We need to get out of here."

"Fine," Luce said as he sat up. The fire was now glowing embers so the only light came from Sandra. Luce looked around. Everyone else was asleep. Luce glanced toward to the forest. Two eyes looked back at him and a chill went through Luce.

"It is time to wake up," Luce called. Tarak and Wyman sat up and looked around. They saw Luce as he started to pack up, but missed seeing the wolf. They started packing as well. Driscoll and Lord Salisbury were slowly getting up. They looked around in confusion.

"It is still dark," Lord Salisbury said, "We should be getting as much sleep as we can."

"We need to get moving," Luce replied, "We cannot stay here any longer."

"Let us get packed up," Driscoll said, "If Luce says we need to get packed up, there is a very good reason."

"At least someone listens to someone," Sandra muttered. Luce ignored the comment and finished packing up his stuff. The rest were soon done as well. When Lord Salisbury grumbled about breakfast, Tarak passed around pieces of dried meat. Wyman lit a lantern before the group headed into the forest because the sun had not yet risen.

The first part of the forest was rough and difficult because they were going through branches and brush, but a little ways in they stumbled on to a path. They could not ride through the brush, so they had to walk their horses.

"A path," Driscoll said, "This may not get us exactly where we are going, but it should get us to the general area if we go to the right."

"Then we might as well get going," Luce said.

They mounted and Wyman led the way with the lantern.

A couple hours later there was enough light filtering through the branches that Wyman was able to put the lantern out and put it away. The forest was mainly deciduous with the occasional conifer. The trees were older, so they were tall and deep rooted. The brush on either side of the path was high and dense. It was impossible to see through to anything on the other side, even the gaps in the bushes showed more bushes that were just as thick. Occasionally a gust of wind would move the leaves. All other noises were muffled and far away.

Luce noticed the leaves were all green as the middle

of summer, but before they had entered the forest the leaves were turning yellow, red, and brown. They had not started falling yet as it had not gotten quite cold enough. He also noticed the path was completely cleaned of any debris from the surrounding plants. Luce reached out with his senses for anything magic related. He expected it all to be dead this close to the portal. Instead he found the trees and plants all had their own magic and there was plenty of it around.

"It is strange," Sandra said from where she was perched on Luce's shoulder, "There is so much magic in what should be a dead zone."

"Maybe not all the magic is gone," Luce said, "Maybe it is all concentrated here."

"Far more likely the forest itself had its own magic," Sandra said, "Most things in nature have a certain amount of magical essence. Those trees have been here long enough to have magic which would not disappear in the same way the rest of the magic did."

"A magical forest?" Driscoll asked, "What does a forest need magic for?"

"To stop it from being cut down," Sandra answered, "Or prevent hunting from within its borders. Some of them just use it to keep out trespassers. But it is hard to tell what exactly this one uses it for."

"Perhaps it uses its magic to keep people from finding the portal," Luce suggested, "After all the portal should not be accessed by just any person, which is why there is a portal guardian. But if the forest itself defends against the average person from stumbling on to it then there is less work for the guardian."

"Then you should have no trouble finding energy,"

Driscoll said.

"But it is not a good idea to try and borrow any of it," Sandra said, "Tree are not known for sharing things."

"And angry trees does not sound good while we are in the middle of the forest," Luce said.

"I see your point," Driscoll said. They were quiet for a minute.

"I was wondering about the man who you think stole the map," Luce said.

"What about him?" Driscoll asked. Tarak and Lord Salisbury started paying attention to the conversation.

"Everything you can tell me," Luce answered.

"He showed up at the city a little more than a year ago," Driscoll said, "Lord Vail brought him to court a week after he arrived. He had been selling potions to the nobility, who believed his claims of youthfulness, weight loss, beautification, healing, and that such. I hoped it was all water, but everyone seems to have survived it. He made his rounds of court selling to everyone who was willing to believe him.

"I remember reading something that talked about the fact that potions no longer worked since the magic had disappeared. So I was not taken in by the man's lies. I would have had him thrown out, but no one else seemed to share my view. I chose not to make those kinds of demands of my people, especially since there have been a few that needed to have their self-image readjusted.

"Then the guards started to find him in places around the castle he should not have been. I warned him after they brought him up from the dungeon. I let Weldon beat him after finding him going through several of the rooms. One of my nobles demanded a duel after the man was found going through his house. The man was scheduled to do so that afternoon when he was found in the throne room inspecting the crown. The guards held him until I got there. I ordered them to search him and all of his belongings. The royal jewel smith was brought in to inspect the crown and make sure that nothing had been done to it. Then I had him escorted to the border of the kingdom and dumped outside it with the threat that if I saw him again I would have him executed."

"Do you know what his name was?" Luce asked.

"Not off the top of my head," Driscoll answered.

"His name was Marlon," Lord Salisbury answered, "There were several rumours about him while he was here."

"Like what?" Luce asked.

"Some people were claiming they saw him and talked to him during times when he was seen someplace else or spoken with someone else," Lord Salisbury answered, "There was also rumours of blackmail, though none was ever found or proven. Someone suggested he was a black wizard, but that was quickly discarded by most because of the disbelief in magic."

"I remember the second time he was in court," Tarak said, "Lord Vail had brought him and they had walked passed me as I was on duty on the gate into the court yard. Lord Vail had decided to walk the few feet from his door to the castle and Marlon went with him. I would have shrugged it off because I did not know anything about him than, but then I saw him again only a few minutes later sneaking into an alley way. I really thought it was strange when he came back out with Lord Vail."

"So, there may have been two of him," Luce said.

"You do not think he was using magic?" Lord Salisbury asked.

"No," Luce answered, "Not unless he had a source of energy. I have had a problem with getting enough energy to do anything. I think it is much more likely that he had a twin."

"Then where did his twin go?" Lord Salisbury asked.

"Probably wherever Marlon is," Luce answered.

"Why are you so interested in Marlon?" Driscoll asked.

"Because I think it is likely that he, or his twin, stole the wizard's skull out of the tower," Luce answered, "And it is much better if the skeleton is buried whole."

"Well, they are long gone by now," Driscoll said, "As far as I know neither have been seen since Marlon was escorted to the border. When we get back I can send out a request to see if anyone has seen Marlon. I would not expect much of an answer though. Proster does not have the best relations with its neighbours."

"It is hard to have good relations when you have neighbours such as Proster does," Luce said.

"What would happen if the wizard is not buried whole?" Lord Salisbury asked.

"Nothing could happen," Luce answered, "Since nothing has happened so far, but occasionally there are repercussions for not burying a wizard whole and they are not pleasant."

"I will send a message to out when we get back,"

Driscoll said. Luce nodded.

"How far along this path should we go?" Wyman asked, turning to look at the group from his position at the front.

"Let me check," Driscoll said as he pulled out a map. He looked it over tracing where he thought they had been with his finger.

"I think we can go along this path for a while longer," Driscoll said, "Maybe for the rest of today."

"That is good," Wyman said, "Because I did not think we could get through the bushes on either side of this path."

"We will figure it out when we need to," Driscoll said, "Though we might be camping on the path tonight."

The group was quiet as they continued. There was very little to see as the trees and bushes looked the same. It made them feel like they really were not getting anywhere even though they had to be moving forward because the path was straight. Wyman kept leading the way and the rest followed with Tarak at the back.

They did not stop for lunch but just ate as they rode. When it was starting to get dark, the worry that they would have to camp in the middle of the path got bigger. However, about the time they were thinking about stopping a clearing became visible. They reached it and found it was an alcove off the path with the bushes around it the same as on the path. In the centre was a marking in the grass as if others had built their fire there. There were plenty of branches and such for fires, which had to be cleaned up anyway if there was going to be space for bedrolls. The clearing was big enough that there was room enough for all five of them had plenty of space.

Everyone set out their bedrolls before Luce built a fire in the spot in the middle of the clearing. Tarak and Wyman used it to make supper. When supper was done the plates were filled and passed around. Once they were finished and everything was cleaned up, they sat there on their bedrolls. None of them felt like going to sleep yet, but they were not sure what to talk about.

"So, what happened with the group once they accepted Lady Erica's request?" Lord Salisbury asked Driscoll.

"Well, they followed the trail," Driscoll said.

After lunch the group headed across the field to the spot where Lady Erica's niece disappeared. They found the marks of goblin feet, footprints of something bigger, and hoof prints from two horses. Todd led the way even though everyone could see the tracks.

The tracks went across the field and into the forest. Again they did not need Todd to lead the way because the traces of the creature's passage was obvious, but they followed him anyway. They went a ways into the forest following this track. Suddenly Todd held up his hand for the group to stop. The tracks went on, but everyone stopped.

"Goblins," Todd said quietly as he took out his bow. Brian got his axe ready. Julie took out her fife. Paul prepared his spells. Sherry took out her dagger. Glenda got ready with her quarterstaff. They made a circle with their backs to each other and facing the trees.

They waited.

The sound of feet reached them. It was the quiet patter of feet on forest floor and it was headed their direction. A minute longer and the ugly faces of the goblins were visible through the branches. The sneering brown faces had scars and pieces missing. The goblins were wielding rusty swords and any other broken, thrown away weapon they could get. They snarled and grunted as they stepped out of the bushes toward the party. The goblins had the group surrounded.

The group stayed where they were and held that position as the goblins got closer. The goblins were only a few feet away when Paul waved his hand and said a few words of magic. The goblins stopped suddenly and looked around in confusion. At that moment the group attacked the goblins. Todd stayed still and fired arrows. Brian went after the goblins swinging. Julie started playing a combination of two songs, one to increase the power of her group and the other to decrease the motivation of the goblins. Sherry did damage to any goblin unfortunate enough to get close to her. Glenda got into the fray with her quarterstaff.

There were plenty of goblins to deal with. It was almost as if someone had cleaned out a nest and sent them out to deal with anyone who wandered into the forest. As the bodies piled up around the group more goblins kept coming. The party did not slow down, or run out of energy as this was what they used to doing. The ground did get a little slippery with goblin blood. Brian slipped and fell on his backside, but he just took out the legs of the goblins around him before getting up to take off their heads.

The fight continued as long as more goblins came at them. They had been fighting a long time and were starting to get tired. The bodies of the dead goblins were starting to get in the way of the battle.

"Drop," Paul shouted. Everyone dropped to the ground without a hesitation. There was a flash of fire and all the goblins became ash. Even the dead bodies disintegrated into ash, but none of the party were injured. Except Glenda, who had to put out her cloak because it had caught on fire. Julie coughed a little as she got to her feet. The rest moved slower to get to the feet. Sherry took out a flask and had a sip before passing it to Brian. He had a pouring before passing it on to Julie. The flask went around the group and back to Sherry, who put the cap on and tucked it away.

"Well, that was fun," Brian said as he wiped down his axe.

"I hope we do not meet another group of enemies that large," Glenda said, "That was almost too many for us to deal with."

"I did not think there was that many goblins in the world," Julie said.

"Maybe someone collected them all together," Sherry said.

"Do we want to meet someone who has collected that many goblins?" Todd asked, "What else has this person collected?"

"We are on our way to find out," Brian answered, "That is the fantastic reason we do this."

"Well, the larger creature continued this way,"

Todd said pointing in the direction they had been going before.

"Since we were not likely expected to survive the goblins we might be able to surprise whoever it is that kidnapped Dawn," Paul said.

"Let us go," Sherry said.

Everyone was ready now, so they continued on. Todd led as he was the one doing the tracking. The creature had not hidden its tracks, so the rest could have followed the trail if they had needed to. They went farther and farther into the forest. It was getting close to evening when they came to a clearing. In the middle of the clearing was a tower. It went up passed the height of the trees and went up double the distance. There was a door at the bottom on the side they came out of the forest. There were no other doors or windows in the tower. The creature's tracks led right to the door, but the door was not big enough to fit anything the size of the tracks.

Sherry went and examined the door. The rest of the group stayed back and waited. They watched as she thoroughly checked the door over. She then did an examination of the rest of the bottom of the tower. When she reached the door again she checked it over a second time. Finally she was satisfied with her inspection and took out her tool kit. She worked on the lock until it clicked and then she pushed in a brick beside the door. The door swung open.

"Come on," Sherry said turning to the group. They followed her through the door and inside the tower. The inside was about twelve feet across with a trap door on the far side of the tower. Sherry was already

checking the trap door as the last of the party entered the tower. Glenda took out a torch and lit it to give Sherry some light.

Once the last person was inside the door closed behind them. Julie tried to open it, but it was locked. Paul tried the door, but it would not budge. He lit a torch and everyone gathered around Sherry. She had made sure that it was safe before pulling it open. The light filtered down to show the staircase, which led to another door at the bottom. Sherry started down the stairs, but held her hand for everyone else to wait up there.

She reached the door, but did not touch it. She studied it for several minutes before looking at the walls on either side of it. Sherry touched the wall on the left side and there was a clack. From there she was able to push the secret door open and stepped through. Everyone was crowded close to the opening in the floor and waited for any response from below. A minute passed before Sherry poked her head out of the secret door.

"Come on down, everyone," Sherry called.

One at a time they went down the stairs and into the secret door. They were all careful not to touch anything else in the stairway. The secret door led to a small hallway with two doors. One at the end and one along the left wall. It was a little cramped with all the people in the hallway. Sherry was already examining the first door on the left. Everyone waited impatiently as she did this. Finally she moved to the second door. She did a quick examination, but apparently found nothing as she opened the door and then dropped to the floor. Nothing happened, so Sherry picked herself up off the floor and led the way into the room."

Driscoll stopped the story as Lord Salisbury started snoring. Tarak and Wyman were also looking like it was pure will that was keeping them awake. Luce was still awake and paying attention.

"I guess that is as far as we get tonight," Driscoll said. He crawled into his bedroll. Tarak and Wyman fell asleep since there was nothing else keeping them awake. Luce thought about keeping a watch, but found himself falling asleep. He did not sense any danger to them, so he gave in and fell asleep.

Luce woke to a prickling on his hand. He looked down at his hand. Sandra was poking him.

"What?" Luce whispered. Sandra did not say anything, but pointed back toward the path. Luce glanced up in that direction. Standing there on the path at the entrance to the clearing was a unicorn. It was completely white and glowed much the same way that Sandra did, where it came from somewhere within the creatures. Its horn shone as if it was made out of silver, but lacked the metallic quality. The unicorn was as large as a war horse with a long, white mane and matching tail. The hoofs were similar in appearance to the horn.

Luce slowly sat up. He tried not to do anything that might scare the creature away. He could not take his eyes off the unicorn. Luce started to lean forward and the unicorn started to back up a little. Luce froze.

"What is it doing here?" Luce whispered to Sandra.

"This is his home," Sandra answered in a whispered, "Where else should he be?"

"I did not think there were any such creatures in this forest," Luce said.

"He is just a shy creature, who is very good at hiding from humans," Sandra said, "I doubt there have been any sightings of unicorns in this forest because if there had been he would be hunted down and killed."

"Could he lead us to the portal?" Luce asked.

"Maybe," Sandra answered. She used her wings to move closer to the unicorn, who stayed still this time. She made some gestures, but did not speak. The unicorn shook its head. Sandra turned back to Luce.

"He says no," Sandra answered, "He knows where it is, but without orders to guide you, he cannot do so. That and he has to stay hidden from the rest of the company for fear they will tell someone he lives here."

"What is he doing here now?" Luce asked, "By showing himself now there is a chance he could be seen by them."

"I do not know," Sandra said. She turned back to the unicorn and once again gestured to it. The unicorn paid attention to her until she was finished, then he turned to Luce.

You will not find what you are looking for along this path, the voice was deep and full of magic, *You must ask for help or you will never find what you are looking for.*

"Ask who for help?" Luce asked.

The unicorn shook his head and then turned away from the clearing toward the path. He looked to be finished his errand and ready to leave, but he looked back one more time. He looked directly at Sandra. She stared at him for a moment.

"What is it?" Luce asked.

"He is asking me to come with him," Sandra answered, "There is something he is hoping I can help him with."

"Go," Luce said.

"But you may need my help," Sandra said.

"You will find us when you are finished," Luce said, "How often do you get a chance to help a unicorn with something?"

"Not very often," Sandra admitted. She flew over to the unicorn and landed on its back. She waved once to Luce and then the unicorn headed down the path. They disappeared around a bend that Luce did not remember the path having.

Luce stayed still for several minutes before he laid down. Something bugged him, so he could not get back to sleep. He sat back up and looked around. There did not seem to be anything to worry about. Luce cast a protection spell around the camp before lying down again. This time he was able to fall asleep without any worries.

It was impossible to tell exactly what time of day it was when Luce woke up, but he was sure that it was shortly before the sun was going to rise. No one else was awake as he sat up. Nothing had disturbed his protection spell, he was just finished sleeping. Since he was not going back to sleep, Luce started to make breakfast. By the time it was ready everyone else was awake and ready to eat.

Less than an hour later they were packed and back on their horses. The path looked the same as it had yesterday. Wyman took the lead again today and Tarak took the rear. Luce checked to see if there was any danger, but there did not seem to be any. He still had not figured out who he was supposed to ask for help from. All the rest of the group had the same idea of where they were going as he did, except for Driscoll maybe.

"How much longer should be follow this path?" Wyman asked as the group started forward.

"An hour or so, I guess," Driscoll answered, "It is hard to tell with the map."

"Okay," Wyman said. He seemed a bit more hesitant today, but that may have been because he was not sure how they were going to leave the path.

The group rode for a while without talking. The scenery was the same as yesterday and did not change much as they went.

"Where did the fairy go?" Driscoll interrupted Luce's thoughts.

"I do not really know," Luce answered, "She said someone needed her help and she would find us when she was finished."

"I have not seen any animals yet in this forest," Driscoll said, "Let alone ones who need help from a fairy, but I suppose if there are any magical creatures we would not get to see them."

"You are likely right," Luce said, "She will be back."

"It is not like we need any help at the moment," Driscoll said, "We are just traveling along this path and hoping to find the place where we can leave it to find the portal. It is fairly boring to do."

"How much farther should we go?" Wyman asked.

"A little farther," Driscoll answered, "Maybe a kilometer or two."

"Yes, sire," Wyman said.

It was a quiet couple kilometers as they searched for any place among the bushes on either side of the path that might be less thick as the rest of it. At the end of the two kilometers they still had not found any spot, but they stopped at the end anyway.

"I guess we just have to do it the hard way," Driscoll said as he got off his horse. The rest of the group got off their horses as well. Driscoll drew his sword and started hacking at the branches to make a path big enough that they could get through. Wyman took the reins of Driscoll horse and then everyone followed Driscoll into the bushes.

It was as dense as it looked and the going was slow. The horses could barely make it through. Driscoll did what he could to clear as much of the brush for everyone else. Eventually he got tired and was having trouble swinging his sword, so Tarak took over cutting through the brush. Tarak was not any faster at it and cleared the same amount of area. He looked to be getting tired as well when he cut through to a clearing of some sort.

Everyone stumbled through after him and found themselves on the path at the exact place they had left it. The hole they had gone through was opposite of the one they had just made. Tiredness swept through the group and they all sat down on the path.

"I guess we get to find out where this path is taking us," Driscoll said, "Apparently it is not going let us leave it."

"Do you think this path leads to the portal?" Lord Salisbury asked.

"No," Luce answered, "But maybe it will lead us to someplace where we can find another way into the forest to search for the portal."

"I hope so," Tarak said as he looked over his sword. His sword and Driscoll's swords were dull from hacking at branches all day. They would have to sharpen them when the group stopped for the night.

While they were sitting there, the group ate lunch. Once they were rested, they climbed back on their horses and continued along the path. The energy was going out of the group. They had not been on this adventure very long and they had not actually run into much danger, but being on a path that might or might not lead them to any place they wanted to go was disheartening. Luce wished he could do something to help out, but anything he tried right now would be shrugged off or make everyone feel worse.

It was that kind of silence in which they rode the rest of the day. Nothing else happened as they rode along the path. About the time it started to get dark they came along another clearing. Luce might have thought it was the same one because it looked the same, but this one was on the other side of the path from the previous one. The group settled into this one just as they had the last clearing.

After supper, Driscoll and Tarak sat there sharpening their swords as Driscoll started into the story.

"So Sherry opened the door and dropped to the ground," Driscoll said, "After getting up, she led the way into the next room.

And the rest followed her inside. This was a larger, circular room with several doors off it and a suit of armour in front of each door. Everyone got their weapons, or method of attack, ready. The suits of armour did not move, or attack them. They lowered their weapons and looked around the room.

"Which one should we try?" Glenda asked.

"How about the closest to the one we just came through?" Paul answered, "And then work our way around."

"Good idea," Glenda said.

Brian and Paul went over to the suit of armour and tried to push it out of the way. Once their hands touched the suit of armour it came alive along with the rest of them causing Paul and Brian jump back. Everyone brought their weapons up to ready. The suits of armour brought their swords up to attack and started toward the group.

Each member of the group picked a suit of armour to attack. Brian's axe barely dented the armour before he was using it to parry with the sword. Julie tried playing a song to cause the armour to lose all magical strength while avoiding the blade of the sword. Paul was using illusions and teleportation spells while hitting the armour with his staff. Sherry's dagger was useless against the armour, so she was dodging the sword while hitting the armour with well-placed kicks. Todd used his short sword to battle the armour. Glenda used her quarterstaff to batter the armour while trying to use a spell that would deal with it.

All the while the suits of armour worked to back them toward the door they had just come in. Glenda managed to get her suit of armour to collapse to the floor and come apart. She moved to on to help Julie, who was closest to her. She engaged the sword, while Julie worked with the song. However, they were both pushed back toward the door. Todd was the first one who was pushed through the doorway. The suit of armour did not follow him out, but made sure he could not come back in. Paul stumbled and was the next one pushed out of the room. Before he could do any magic to get back in, Sherry ended up on top of him causing him land on his backside. Glenda and Julie were the next ones pushed out of the room and back into the cramped hallway. Brian was still swinging his axe and parrying the sword, but was getting overwhelmed as two other suits of armour had joined the fight and were forcing him to back up. He too was pushed through the doorway. Once he was on the other side of it, the door closed in his face. The group found themselves in the hallway with the suits of armour on the other side of the closed door.

"That did not go well," Paul said, "What should we try next?"

"Magic worked for one," Glenda said, "That means there is one less to fight when we go back in. The spell was for taking magic out of animated objects."

"I know something similar," Paul said.

"Then fighters in front," Julie said, "Spell casters in the back. We see what we can do while the armour is

distracted by the fight."

"Good idea," Paul said.

Brian, Todd, and Sherry sorted themselves into a sort of line in the front, while Paul, Glenda, Julie did the same for a line behind. When they were sorted out, Brian opened the door. He was the first one through with Todd and Sherry right behind. They stood there ready for combat, but the suits of armour were all back to their positions in front of the doors. Even the one Glenda had taken down.

They froze and looked around in confusion. Paul, Glenda, and Julie had not come through the door, but they looked through the doorway at the suits of armour.

"What happened?" Brian asked.

"It reset," Paul answered, "Someone has to go touch one of them to get them to attack again."

"That is easy enough," Brian said. He walked over to the one closest to him and touched it before moving back to his position in the line. The suits of armour started moving again. Once again they attacked. Brian, Todd, and Sherry worked at keeping the suits of armour concentrated on them. It meant each of them were fighting two suits each. The suits of armour were working to push them back out of the room.

The rest of the group worked to cast the spells necessary to make the suits of armour to collapse. Since they did not have to dodge the swords this time it was easier for them to concentrate and get the spells right.

They had managed to get three of the suits down when the fighters were pushed back out of the room and the door closed. Brian's axe ended up in the middle of the door because he tried to prevent it from closing.

"Well, that did not work," Sherry said, "Next suggestion."

The group was silent as they rested. Brian pulled his axe out of the door. There was a mark left on it, but the door was still intact.

"The spells work," Paul said, "They caused the suits of armour to collapse."

"If we do managed to beat them, we are just going to have to fight them the next time we are through the room," Glenda said.

"Maybe there is a way to take out the suit of armour in front of the door we want to go through," Todd asked.

"We can try it," Paul said, "After all, they did not attack until after they were touched."

"Let's go," Brian said getting up. He opened the door and stepped into the room. Sherry and Todd followed him with the other three behind them. Brian stopped near the suit of armour they had tried to move earlier and positioned himself at ready. Sherry and Todd took their positions facing the other suits of armour. Glenda stood behind Brian and got ready to cast the spell. Paul and Julie stood nearby to assist her if needed. Glenda cast the spell. The suit of armour collapsed and the pieces scattered. None of the rest of the suits of armour moved.

Sherry moved passed the pieces of armour and checked over the door. Once she was sure that it was safe, she unlocked it. She opened it and stepped inside. The rest... of... the... group... followed..."

Driscoll was falling asleep as he was telling the story. He lost the fight to stay awake and his head rested on his chest. Lord Salisbury helped him lie down and put a cover over him. The rest of the group climbed into their own bedrolls and laid down. Luce cast the protection spell before closing his eyes and going to sleep.

Luce was the first awake the next morning. He made breakfast, which was ready by the time everyone else was up. They packed up camp and mounted their horses. Once again they started along the path, which at this point seemed endless.

About the time they were thinking about lunch, Wyman called out that there was something on the path ahead. Everyone looked up to see a squirrel skitter from one side of the path to the other.

"That is the first animal I have seen," Driscoll said.

"There are more of them," Luce said, "If you listen you can hear them." The group was quiet for a minute. They could hear the squirrels chattering to each other.

"That sounds like a lot of squirrels," Tarak said, "I think we should be careful."

"I agree," Luce said. They all dismounted and drew their swords. Then they started forward again.

"Squirrels cannot be that bad, can they?" Driscoll asked.

"They have teeth and claws," Luce answered, "Those make them dangerous enough without the fact that they are small, which makes them hard to kill."

The book dropped to the floor and Mitchell's head fell to his chest. His eyes would no longer stay open. The fire was burning down and it was getting too dark to read by. The oil lamps had burned themselves out and would need to be refilled. The house was quiet except for the creak of it settling and the ticking of the mantle clock.

ADVENTURES IN THE FOREST AND ADVENTURES IN THE DUNGEON OF THE TOWER

Mitchell shook himself awake. He was not sure how long he had been sleeping, but it was dark in the room. Even the embers had stopped glowing. Mitchell got up and went to the window. Pulling back the curtains, he found that it was still dark outside. He used the small amount of light from the street lamp to get the fire ready. When it was built up, he lit it. It started slowly, but grew quickly. Mitchell closed the curtain and went back to his chair. The book lay on the floor. He picked it up and flipped through it until he came to the page had been on.

"Squirrels cannot be that bad, can they?" Driscoll asked.

"They have teeth and claws," Luce answered,

"Those make them dangerous enough without the fact that they are small, which makes them hard to kill."

No one said anything else as they moved forward.

They reached the spot where they had seen the squirrel and found the path looked the same there as it had appeared all the way along. They could still hear the squirrels, but could not see any. They continued forward. As if they crossed an invisible line on the path, suddenly the squirrels stopped chattered and appeared on the branchs of the bushes on both sides of the path. They all looked angry and dangerous. The group stopped and looked around. Both sides stood as if waiting for the signal. Lord Salisbury's horse bucked and pulled the reins away from Lord Salisbury. As it was running off down the path, the squirrels took that as a signal to attack.

All five of them found it easy to skewer the squirrel on their swords, but they had to be quick about cleaning them off. A dozen or more squirrels attacked each person at once. Luce found he could burn up one with a small fireball while skewering another with his sword. He still had to brush them off him before he could do either attack. He, like the rest of the group, was collecting small bite marks all over his body. With some finesse he managed to protect certain parts of his body from the squirrels, but it cost him some of his ability to kill them faster.

Driscoll had taken out his dagger to use as a second weapon. He worked to get one of each and then cross them to clean them off before getting two more. His reflexes were fast, but they were not as fast as the squirrels. Driscoll was also trained to kill men not small animals, which made things more difficult. He managed to keep the squirrels out of his clothing, but otherwise he was getting bitten everywhere.

Tarak and Wyman were slowed down by their armour, which the squirrels were managing to get inside. They were killing as many as they could while trying to shed the armour, which was no help in this fight anyway. Lord Salisbury had an easier time, but he had started slicing through as many squirrels as he could in one swing instead of skewering them on the end of his sword. He killed more in one strike, but he could also end up missing all the squirrels he was aiming at.

The squirrels were not infinite and had stopped appearing out of the bushes, but there was still a large amount for each person to deal with. Luce used a stronger spell that caused his whole body to heat up and burn the ones on him to ash. Then he went back to skewering and burning the ones around him. Driscoll kept going with his method of attack, as did the other three. Luce ran out of squirrels first and moved to help Driscoll out. They managed to get all those around and on Driscoll. Both moved to help the other three, who were suffering the worst because they could not find ways to keep the squirrels from getting into their clothing. Luce could not use the spell to burn the squirrels on the others because it would burn them as well. Instead he and Driscoll thumped the squirrels with the flat of their blades and the others would have to shake the squirrels out from there.

Finally all the squirrels were corpses lying on the path. They bandaged the worst of the bites before moving on to other things. Luce pushed them all into a pile in the middle of the path, while the others worked to make sure they did not have any more in their clothing or armour. Then Tarak and Wyman put their armour back on and Lord Salisbury found his horse. The horse had not gotten far, but it still needed calming down. Once everyone was ready to move on, Luce reduced the corpses to a pile of ash. Then the group moved forward.

They were much more wary as they continued, but they did not see any more creatures as they went. They ate a small lunch without stopping. The afternoon went by quietly as they rode along the endless path to a destination they were not sure about on a quest that three of them did not understand. Luce tried telling a couple jokes, but they fell flat, despite Driscoll's attempts to laugh at them.

As it was starting to get dark another clearing came into view, this one on the opposite side of the path from the last one. It was identical in all other aspects. They made camp the same as before. It was pretty much down to a routine to the point as soon as supper was cleaned up Driscoll sat on his bedroll and waited for everyone to be quiet before he started the next part of the story.

"The rest of the group followed Sherry into this room.

The room was square with a door on the opposite side. There was a table in the middle of the room with clay bowls and plates along with some cutlery. There was no food though. On the walls on either side of this room were several shelves, which had boxes and other such that suggested a place to eat, except that there was no food anywhere in there. On the top shelves were four gargoyles, one at each corner. The group was watchful of them, but none of them moved as the group entered the room.

The group shuffled along to the centre of this room on their way to the door on the other side. They got half way there when the gargoyles came to life and swooped down on them. The group already had their weapons out and were ready for them.

Brian's axe connected to the one that attacked him. It took a large chip out of the stone creature, but did not slow down the gargoyle itself. He was able to take several more swings at it while avoiding the claws that wanted to rip his flesh apart. Sherry and Todd took on the one that tried to attack her. It managed to scrap its claw across her shoulder as she went into a roll to avoid it, but otherwise it missed her. Todd chopped at it with his sword. Sherry banged it with her fists, feet, and knife.

Paul used a spell that made the gargoyle have difficulty hitting them because it was aiming at an image of them which was slightly off from where he and Glenda were standing. Glenda was doing damage to the stone with her quarterstaff. Julie was dealing with the last gargoyle by hypnotizing it with a song, which was working quite well. The gargoyle had not attacked her and was instead standing there swaying to the music Julie was playing on her fife.

Brian hit the gargoyle hard enough with his axe that the head flew off and smashed against the wall. The *rest of the body collapsed without the head. Todd and Sherry were doing small amounts of damage to theirs, but they kept working on it.*

Glenda had smacked the gargoyle into the wall, which caused it to crumble a little. Paul was trying some word puzzles, but aside from some minor chips they did not seem to be doing much. Julie had her gargoyle falling into a deep sleep it probably would not be waking up from.

Brian gave Todd and Sherry a hand with theirs. When he landed a blow with his axe there was a chip out of the gargoyle, but not much more damage than that. He had swung for another blow when all the gargoyles exploded into dust. Brian was barely able to stop his swing and turn away from the gargoyle to avoid getting a mouthful of dust. Todd was not quite so lucky. Sherry had been rolling to avoid another attack and did not get the dust in her face.

Julie was far enough away from her gargoyle that she was safe from the dust. Paul was also far enough to miss it, but Glenda breathed in some. She and Todd coughed the dust back as they tried to clear their airways.

"What happened?" Julie asked.

"I think it was one of my word puzzles," Paul said, "I was not quite expecting a result quite that strong."

"A little warning would be nice for next time," Glenda said between coughing fits. Paul took out his water skin and offered her a drink. She accepted it. Todd had taken out his own water skin to use to clear his mouth. The rest of the group dusted themselves off.

Once everyone was ready, Sherry went to the door

at the end of the room and checked it over.

"It is clear," Sherry said.

"Then let us see what it there," Glenda said. She opened the door and stepped inside. The rest followed her. It was a small square room with a design painted on the floor. Sherry started checking the walls for any other way out of there. Paul looked over the design painted on the floor.

"A creation glyph," Paul said, "The person puts the object in the centre and says the correct spell. The object is then animated and is useful for defending his lab."

"Why have it here?" Julie asked, "Why not farther into his lab?"

"Unless it was easier to bring the objects in here, I do not know," Paul answered, "I would also think this is something to have farther into the lab."

"There is nothing else in this room," Sherry said.

"Nothing else to effect the spell," Paul said.

"So, next door back at the room full of armour?" Brian asked.

"Might as well," Paul answered, "There is nothing else here."

The group put their weapons away and left the small room. They went back through the room with gargoyle dust on the floor. Exiting that room to be back in the circular room, there was no suit of armour in front of the door. The suit of armour was not lying in pieces on the floor either. It had moved to stand in front of the door leading out of this place.

"I wonder if they attacked whether they would push back into the room we just came out of," Brian said,

"Or back through the first door."

"Let us not find out," Sherry said as she moved toward the door to their right with everyone else.

"I was just wondering," Brian said, "I was not actually going to do anything which would cause us to find out." He caught up with the rest of the group and pushed his way to his position at the front. They faced the next suit of armour standing guard in front of the door they wanted."

Lord Salisbury and Tarak were starting to snore. Wyman's head was sinking down to the sleep position. Driscoll got into his bedroll and went to sleep himself. Luce sat there long enough to put the protection spell in place before he climbed into his bedroll.

The next day had a morning routine similar to the last few days. The path was the same as always. As much as they should have been watchful, everyone in the group had turned their thoughts inward.

It was easy to get discouraged along this path. Nothing changed. The trees were still green and full leafed. The path was still brown dirt moist enough not to become dust. What could be seen of the sky was blue with a few clouds. The light shifted as the day went on, but otherwise stayed in the same place. The path was straight, but it was hard to see anything ahead, or behind them. There did not seem to be any end to it all.

Three grizzly bears dropped out of nowhere with no warning, causing the horses to rear up. Driscoll and Tarak stayed on their horses, but the other three were thrown. Luce picked himself up and drew his sword. He looked up at the bear standing on its hind legs over him and ready for the attack. The second bear was busy clawing at Wyman, who had still lay where he had fallen. It was hard to tell if he was dead, or just pretending in hope that the bear would leave him alone. Driscoll was still mounted as he tried to take off the bear's head as he rode pass. The bear dropped to get closer to Wyman and the swing missed it. Lord Salisbury had not gotten up either, but Tarak had dismounted to take on the third bear and prevent it from getting to Lord Salisbury.

The bear was close to mauling Wyman when Wyman shoved his sword through the beast's throat and pulled it out through the side. The bear collapsed on top of Wyman. Driscoll dismounted and pulled the bear's body off him. Wyman coughed a couple times before letting Driscoll help him to his feet.

Luce kept the bear at arm's length with his sword, which meant that he avoided injury, but did not have to power to thrust the sword into it. Driscoll and Wyman attacked the bear from the other side. It fought for several minutes before it was brought down by overwhelming odds. The three of them moved to where Tarak was doing what he could to keep the bear away from Lord Salisbury, who still had not moved. Lord Salisbury was awake and scared, but did not make any attempt to get off the ground.

The last bear did not have a chance against all four of the men and collapsed from multiple blows. It made one moan and then all that was left was the corpse. Wyman and Tarak went to round up the horses. While Luce and Driscoll went over to Lord Salisbury, who still had not moved.

"Is there not a spell you can use to control the animals?" Driscoll asked.

"I never studied animal control," Luce answered, "I have never been an animal person. Thus I do not have any spells to control animals."

"Well, they would be useful about now," Driscoll said.

"Maybe I can find someone to teach me a couple for next time," Luce said, "But for now we just have to deal with the animals as they show up."

"It seems like a waste to kill them like this," Driscoll said.

"You can take some meat to cook for later, if you want," Luce said.

"No," Driscoll shook his head, "It does not feel appropriate." Driscoll turned to Lord Salisbury.

"What is wrong?" Driscoll asked.

"Shooting pains through my arm," Lord Salisbury answered, "I think it is broken."

"I am going to take a look," Luce said.

"Go ahead," Lord Salisbury said. Luce felt along the arm and Lord Salisbury winced when Luce got close to the wrist. Luce carefully rolled up the sleeve of Lord Salisbury's shirt and jacket. Just before the wrist the arm looked twisted.

"We are going to have to find someone with medical training," Driscoll said, "If any of us try to splint that it is not going to heal properly."

"I have a way to do a small amount of help," Luce said. He waved his hand over the area and spoke the words of a spell. The arm straightened itself out. Lord

Salisbury prepared himself for the pain, but relaxed when none came.

"It is healed?" Driscoll asked.

"Not all the way," Luce answered, "But it painlessly straightened it and started the bone along the healing process. We should still put a splint on it and it should be used as little as possible. Anything else that hurts?"

"I cannot feel any," Lord Salisbury answered. He was slow to sit up as he was cautious about something else have been broken. He managed to get to his feet without any other issues. By the time he was up, Tarak and Wyman brought back the horses.

They stopped to have a little bit of lunch before they mounted the horses and got ready to continue on. Nothing else happened until they reached another clearing for the night.

The only person who did not help set up camp was Lord Salisbury, because everyone else refused to let him. Supper was cooked, eaten, and then cleaned up. Finally everyone got ready to hear another installment of the story.

"So, they knew what worked to get through the doors on the other sides of the suits of armour," Driscoll said, "This made it easy for them to figure out how to get through the next one.

Brian took the front position with Sherry and Todd while everyone else stayed behind them. Glenda cast the spell this time and the suit of armour collapsed just as the previous one had. Sherry stepped around the pieces to check over the door. Apparently the only guard on it was the suit of armour, because she opened the door and went inside. The rest of the group followed.

The room was about the length for both of the previous rooms combine, but it was wider. There was an altar on a dais at the end farthest from the door with a carpet going from one to the other. On both sides of the carpet there were eight stone pillars.

The group slowly went further into the room, but there did not appear to be any enemies. Brian took a firm grip on his axe and headed down the carpet. The rest of the group cautiously followed him.

Other than the altar there was nothing else in the room. There was nothing on the alter, except a design painted on top. Brian went all the way around it while everyone else, except Paul, waited off the dais. Paul studied the design.

"It is for summoning creatures," Paul said after a few minutes.

"Can we destroy it?" Brian asked.

"Go ahead," Paul answered stepping back from the altar.

"Fantastic," Brian said as he got ready to swing. His axe smashed through it without trouble. Brian continued until the altar was reduced to kindling. Then Brian raked the pieces all together and then stepped back. Paul stepped forward and said a spell of the wood, which caused them to burst into flame. Everyone stood there and watched until the fire had burned all the wood. Brian stamped out the rest before it could set anything else on fire.

Then everyone turned to leave only to stop in their tracks. The pillars had turned into statues and were coming toward the group with sharp looking swords. The party of adventures took out their weapons.

"Any useful spells?" Sherry asked, "Or at least any way to make it a more evenly matched fight."

"It depends on what they are made of," Paul answered.

"What about the spell you used that turned the gargoyles to dust?" Julie asked.

"I would have to figure out which word puzzle it was that had the effect," Paul said, "It was one of three puzzles that I used."

"You figure it out while we distract them," Brian said.

"I am working on it," Paul said. He stayed where he was and the rest of the group moved closer to the statues. Julie started playing her fife, but the song had no apparent effect on the statues. Glenda tried a spell of her own, but it did not work either. Brian charged with his axe and Todd went with his sword in hand. Whatever the statues were made out of was much harder than anything they had encountered before. They were not even getting the statues to chip and definitely not taking off any body parts.

"I think I got it," Paul said. Brian and Todd backed away from the statues. Paul spoke a jumble of words that did not make any sense. The statues froze, but they did not turn to dust.

"So, it works different depends on the material?" Brian asked.

"One way to find out," Sherry answered. She went toward the statues. They did not move. She went passed them without incident. Sherry got as far as the door

and opened it. The statues remained froze.

"Let us get out of here before they come back to life," Glenda said. The group walked carefully passed the statues. They made it to the door and through without the statues coming to life. Once again the suit of armour had moved to a different door. Glenda used a salve to seal the door. She etched some symbols in the salve. Then the group turned their attention to the next door.

Luce found himself nodding off as Driscoll finished this piece of the story. He was barely aware when Driscoll stopped and got into his bedroll. Luce let his eyes close and he was asleep.

Luce was the first one awake the next morning. The routine was the same, but Lord Salisbury was careful of his arm and sat out of it all. Aside from Lord Salisbury, everyone else was getting faster as getting everything together, which meant they were on the path faster. And feeling like they were not getting anywhere despite spending more time on the path.

Tarak and Wyman were watchful of anything that might attack the group, while the rest sunk into their own thoughts. It was much easier to do this than it was to think up topics of conversation, or jokes, or anything similar. Luce had no idea what was ahead and he had always planned to travel this path alone. Driscoll had volunteered himself and through him, his guards. He had no idea what to expect on an adventure, but he always thought it would be more exciting than this. Lord Salisbury was just glad the weather was not colder because he had not taken the time to pack properly and he did not have the proper clothing for when winter hit. That and he had used his third shirt as a sling when he only had packed three.

They did not stop for lunch, but just ate their rations as they rode. There were not exactly any places to stop and none of them wanted to anyway. If they stopped it would slow down the journey and even if they were not getting anywhere it was better to get there faster.

In the middle of the afternoon when Wyman sat up straighter in the saddle and held up his hand to stop the group. The group stopped which made them quiet because the horses had been making the only sounds. Everyone listened for whatever sound that caused Wyman to halt. The only noises reaching them were the same muffled ones they always heard. Wyman stayed still a few moments longer with nothing happening.

Wyman got off his horse and signalled for everyone else to do the same, which they did. Wyman handed his reins back. Lord Salisbury took them as well as the reins of the others horses. He took all the horses back to behind where Tarak had been before he moved up to where Wyman was.

Everyone got their weapons out and got ready to deal with whatever was going to attack them. They started forward. As if they crossed an invisible line on the path a cougar came out of the brush one either side of the path. With the two opponents on the ground they almost missed the two cougars crawling out on branches over the path. As the ones on the ground attacked the two in the trees dropped down on top of the group.

Luce swung at the closest cougar, but it dodged out of the way. Then he had to dodge the cougar's attack on him. Everyone else was dealing with the same thing. Luce worked to keep the cougar out of the range of its paw while still within in the reach of his sword. The rest were trying to do the same. None of them were succeeding very well.

Luce searched for any spells that might help them out of this situation. Most of his spells did not involve attacking anything and his fire spell was limited. He had sleep spells, warmth spells, light spells, noise spells, cleaning spells, and that such. None of them were applicable to this situation. The cougar launched itself at Driscoll, knocking him down, and biting at his neck. Lord Salisbury jumped into action and used his sword one handed as he sliced at the cougar. The cougar was too focused on Driscoll and did not notice Lord Salisbury until the sword bit into its flesh. Lord Salisbury ripped the cougar's side wide open. The cougar made a meowing noise before collapsing on top of Driscoll. Lord Salisbury pushed the cougar off Driscoll before offering Driscoll a hand up. Driscoll accepted it and got to his feet without anything more than some scratches. He got ready to attack again.

Luce tried the spell to make a loud noise. The cougars backed off a little bit, but then growled and attacked. Luce thought about it a little longer and then decided to try the sleep spell. The cougars staggered a little, but only the one to actually fall asleep was the one Luce was fighting. He put his sword through more by accident than on purpose as it collapsed to the ground. Luce pulled his sword out.

While the last two cougars were fighting off the spell, the group attacked them and was finally able to bring them down. Once they were sure that the cougars were dead, they rolled them into the bushes. Tarak did a thorough examination of Driscoll before they could continue. Finally they remounted their horses and rode onward.

"Ever get the feeling that we are not welcome here?" Driscoll asked Luce, "Because the attacks from the animals are very strange and out their nature."

"I noticed that," Luce said, "They are also strangely resistant to magic. The magic of the forest likely has something to do with it all."

"So, it might be using the magic to tell us that it does not like trespassers?" Driscoll asked.

"Yes," Luce answered.

"We should not be here then," Lord Salisbury said.

"What else do you think the forest will send to attack us?" Driscoll asked Luce.

"Any animals native to the area," Luce answered.

"That is a lot of varieties," Driscoll said.

"Unless we can figure some way off this path," Luce said.

"What about going back?" Lord Salisbury asked.

"Do you think that magic that makes sure we cannot go either direction on the sides, will let us go back the way we came?" Luce asked, "Do you think that if you do go back, you will find the place where we came on to this path?"

"So, forward?" Lord Salisbury asked.

"Until a better plan comes along," Driscoll answered.

No one said anything else as they rode on, but the mood went farther down. Lord Salisbury and the guards were wondering if they were ever going to get out of this. Luce and Driscoll thought about what else the forest would get to attack them tomorrow.

The clearing arrived for them to camp in for the night. They made up camp, had supper, and then sat around the fire.

"The group turned their attention to the next door and the suit of armour that stood in front of it," Driscoll started,

Brian once again took the front with Paul casting the spell from behind. The suit of armour clattered to the ground and Sherry stepped forward. Once she had checked over the door, Sherry opened it and stepped inside. Brian followed her and the rest of the group went in after him.

This room was about twenty feet by twenty feet with stone walls. There was a table and chairs in the centre, but that was all that was in the room, except for a pile of bones below the table. The bones looked like they had been nibbled clean; however, it was hard to tell how long ago that was. Aside from all that there were insects sketched on to the walls. Each insect was about a hand length long and about half as wide. They looked similar to a beetle, but there was strange markings on the bugs.

"This is interesting," Paul said, "I would also say that these were ortell beetle, but ortell beetles have a slightly different markings."

"They looked like they are metal with the sharp

corners," Julie said.

"They do have that look," Paul said.

"Every room has had an enemy in it," Brian said, "Those bugs are the only thing I can see that could attack, unless the table is going to come alive. How do we deal with metal bugs? Especially since there is so many of them?"

"What are some of the traits of ortell beetles?" Glenda asked.

"They are a magical bug," Paul answered, "They have to be crushed because if they are split each piece remakes itself into two separate bugs. Their shell is hard and their bite is poisonous. If you freeze they are likely to ignore you, or become uninterested."

"I guess that is a good start is how to deal with them," Brian said, "But what triggers them?"

"If we have not triggered them, then maybe we can leave without having to fight them," Sherry suggested, "We do not have to fight everything we come across."

"The statues were triggered when we tried to leave the other room," Brian said, "Maybe that is what we need to get the beetles to trigger."

Sherry went back to the door and tried to open it. It would not open, so she tried a few ways to get it open. None of it worked.

"Apparently we cannot get out," Sherry said, "And it did not trigger the bugs."

"Perhaps just touching the beetles," Paul suggested. Everyone got ready while Paul reached out toward the beetle he had been studying. His fingers reached it and he brushed them across it. The beetle did not come alive, neither did any of the other ones.

"*So, that is not how to trigger them,*" *Glenda said,* "*There must be something around here that is meant to trigger the beetles.*"

The group started wandering the room and poking at any places that might have been the trigger to making the beetles come alive. Brian was near the table when he heard a clicking sound. He looked underneath it and found a live beetle crawling around on the bottom it. He swatted it and it flew a few feet to land in front of Todd. Todd lifted his foot and started to stomp on the bug. The beetle made some more clicking sounds before it went crunch.

The bugs on the walls started to come alive. They were exactly as they looked when they were just pictures, except they were darker than the stone of the walls and the markings were in black. Each one took a few seconds to orient itself before heading toward Todd. Every member of the group started stomping on any beetle that they could. It was like a mad dance with the sounds of crunching beetles as the music.

Sherry missed a beetle and it managed to crawl up her leg. She tried to swat it away, but it moved too fast. She tried again and it clung to her sleeve. The beetle bit her wrist before she could get it off and stomp on it. She continued to stomp on the beetles, along with everyone else.

Finally all the beetles were smashed bits on the floor and everyone was cleaning off their shoes.

"*Anyone hurt?*" *Glenda asked.*

"*I got bit,*" *Sherry answered.*

"*What kind of poison is it?*" *Glenda asked Paul.*

"*Habituopiate,*" *Paul answered, "It is usually dealt*

with using a universal antidotes."

"I have one of those," Glenda said going through her bag, "Somewhere." It took her a few minutes to find it.

"Here it is," Glenda said taking it out. She used it on Sherry's wrist before bandaging the bite and then getting Sherry to take a sip to make sure all the poison was neutralized.

Once Glenda was done, Julie went to the door. The door opened easily for her and she went through into the room with the suits of armour. Everyone else followed her out."

Driscoll stopped at that point even though everyone was still awake and listening. When he finished, all of them got into their bedrolls and lied down. Luce put the protection spell up before letting himself fall asleep.

Luce sat up and looked around. Something had woken him, but he could not identify it. Whatever it was did not happen again. Luce felt around inside the protection spell and did not find anything. He felt around the edges of the protection spell, but there was nothing there now. Luce looked around the clearing, but he did not see anything in the blackness of the night. The fire had died down and did not provide any light. Any light was what filtered down from the stars. But nothing moved from what little Luce could see. He lied back down and tried to go back to sleep. Sleep did not come, but he did not move anyway.

It was not until Wyman started moving that Luce sat up again. The sky had lightened some by this time and they could see a lot farther. There was nothing to be seen that concerned them. So, they started breakfast. Everyone else woke up as breakfast was being cooked.

After the usual morning routine, they were mounted and headed down the path. The path was the same as was everything else, but something felt different. Luce could feel the difference, but it took him a while to figure out what the feeling was. It was the feeling of being followed. However, Luce could not figure out what or who it was. He tried to see the person, but nothing could be seen behind them. He had tried magic, but whoever it was blocked from his senses. However, it was not one spot that was blocked instead it was as if there was nothing there at all.

Wyman had noticed the feeling, but ignore it to focus on what was in front of the group. Tarak, however, was constantly looking over his shoulder as if trying to catch a look at the person behind him. Driscoll seemed not to notice any of this, but it was more likely that he left the watching to his guards so they would not think he did not trust them to do their jobs. Lord Salisbury was nervous though he tried to replicate Driscoll's unconcern. As usual they did not stop for lunch and ate while they rode.

They still had not seen who was following them, but it was Wyman started paying more attention to what was in front of them. Luce attention was also drawn to the path in front as this was about the usual time that they were attacked by animals. He had spent some time thinking over what sort of animal might attack them today. There were too many possibilities for him to narrow things down. So far they had been attacked by two larger animals and one smaller animal. Since Luce knew that there were magical beasts in the forest as well, that left a lot of possible animals that could attack them.

They must have crossed the invisible line because crows started to swoop down and attack them. All of them had swords which were useless unless a crow was busy attacking someone else and did not see to dodge out of the way. Luce started using his fire spell to target the crows, which worked well enough because there was some many of them. If he missed one he would hit another. The crows started to target him and for every one he managed to take out another one would join the attack. Luce had to duck his head and use his arms to cover it. The others tried their best to help him out with slashing at the crows with their swords. This took out a few more crows because the crows were too busy to dodge the attacks.

Once he could lift his head, Luce shot the fire spell at the larger group and destroyed a handful of them before he had to duck again. The others swung at the crows again. This went for several rounds with it seemed like more crows joining the fight and never enough losses for there to be holes in the ranks. A few rounds more and it appeared that the crows were running out of replacements. This gave the men more energy to fight the crows. Luce felt very fortunate to have found the amulet because otherwise he would have run out of energy long ago and probably have been pecked to death.

When they reached the point of only a handful of crows things got more complicated. They continued to attack Luce, but the others were having trouble hitting the crows without hitting Luce, who was having difficulty aiming the fire spell before he had to duck again. They did continue to deal with a few though. As the number of crows got smaller, it became harder and harder to hit them. At five, no one had been able to hit one in several rounds, except Luce and his fire spell, which had only taken one out. It was hard to take out any more crows because they were faster, paid more attention, and there too few.

After a few more rounds of zero causalities, Luce changed the spell a little bit so that it would go after the crows before releasing it. This time the spell got two crows and Tarak got one that dodged out of the way of the spell. The next casting got one of the crows, but it took a third casting before the last one was dead. They checked themselves over, but aside from some falling ash they were fine. They continued along the path.

"Crows," Driscoll said, "What else can the forest threaten us with?"

"I am not sure," Luce answered, "Any creature residing in the forest, I would guess."

"Between the animals who are attacking us and the person who is following us, you would think that we really were not welcome here," Driscoll said.

"The sooner we get out of here the happier I will be," Lord Salisbury said.

"We will make it out of here," Driscoll said, "This path has to lead to somewhere."

"We have been going along it for several days now and there has not been any paths off it," Lord Salisbury said, "It has not turned, but gone straight. Yet we cannot see what is behind us, or in front of us."

"I doubt it goes on forever," Driscoll said, "It just seems like it right now."

Lord Salisbury shrugged in response and that was the end of the conversation for the afternoon.

As usual they came upon a clearing when it was time to camp. Luce put two protection spells on the camp before they ever started to get settled. Then they all worked to get the camp set up and supper ready. When supper was cleaned up, they sat around the fire ready to listen to another piece of the story.

"They faced the next suit of armour and deal with the same as the other ones," Driscoll started.

Sherry did her usual check of the door before opening it. Everyone followed her inside. This room was as long and as wide as the last one. This one had smooth, unmarked walls and a dirt floor. There was nothing in this room. No furniture, or crates, or anything. The group stayed near the door for the moment.

"I do not see anything that looks like it could be an enemy," Brian said.

"I do not see anything in here at all, except for a bare room," Sherry said. Both of them took a step forward. Nothing happened.

"Maybe we should go to the next room," Julie suggested. Paul tried the door.

"It locked behind us," Paul said, "We might as well go forward, though it does not look like anything is there." The rest of the group turned back to the room as Brian and Sherry took another few steps forward.

Todd moved up to be in line with Brian and Sherry as they moved forward.

"Be careful," Glenda said as she, Paul, and Julie also started forward, but at a much slower pace. They spread out so that they could examine the whole room as they went. Brian, Sherry, and Todd continued forward. There did not seem to be any danger, or any enemies. There did not seem to be anything that would, could, harm them.

Brian stepped on something and there was a brief clicking sound before the ground gave out beneath him, Sherry and Todd. They slide with a yelp and a scream down several feet to stone floor. The other three rushed forward, but stopped just before falling into the pit. Paul's foot hit something that made a brief clicking sound. This time an iron gate fell from the ceiling and the three barely jumped back out of the way. The points of the bars dropped up to the first bar into the ground and did not look like they would be easy to pull up. The squares were too small for anyone to fit through.

"Is everyone all right?" Paul asked the other two.

"Yes," Glenda replied.

"I am okay," Julie answered. Paul went over to the iron gate.

"Is everyone down there all right?" Paul called down.

"We are fine," Sherry called back.

"Maybe a little sore on our back ends," Brian said.

"We cannot get to you," Paul said, "Because of the iron bars. Is there any way out of that pit?"

"Just a minute," Sherry called back. She took out a torch and lit it before looking around. There was a

tunnel that went in the direction that the door was up top and the other direction was a blank wall. The tunnel narrowed to the point where one person could walk, but two people across would be a really tight fit. It was dark so it was impossible to see how far it went, or whether there was anything at the other end.

"There is a tunnel down here," Sherry called up, "We can probably get out that way if we are careful. Can you get out?"

"I do not know," Paul said, "Just a minute."

Julie went over to the door and tried it. The door opened without difficulty.

"Yes, we can get out," Paul called back.

"Then we will find you once we find a way out," Sherry called.

"We will wait in the room with the suits of armour," Paul called back.

"Okay," Sherry said.

Paul, Glenda, and Julie headed into the other room. While below Sherry took the lead down the tunnel. Brian had taken out his own torch, so he took the rear. The tunnel was stone with dirt tracked in from the room above. Somewhere there was water because there was moisture causing moss to grow on the walls and the dirt to be damp.

The tunnel kept going. It went much farther than they thought was from the one room to the room with the suits of armour. And it kept going from there. They had gone far enough that the tower was likely a ways behind them and still continued. They stopped briefly for a drink of water. They continued along the tunnel without meeting anything else along the way.

Finally they reached another room. This one was small round and appeared to have nowhere to go. They crowded into the room and looked around. There appeared to be no way out, but there was a switch on the wall beside the doorway. Sherry checked it over for any traps, but did not find any. She touched it. There was a beep and then the floor started upward taking the three of them with it. They worked to stabilize themselves to avoid falling down. The floor went up several levels before it stopped. The walls had changed from stone to looking like the inside of the tree. There was a door was in the same side. Sherry checked the door before letting Brian open it. The other side of the door was just forest.

Sherry and Todd followed Brian out. They all looked around.

"The tower is that way," Brian said pointing the direction they had come from.

"Apparently that was just to get the people to leave," Sherry said, "Let us head back. It should be easy to get to the tower from here."

"Yup," Brian said. They headed for the tower, which was visible through the trees. The time it took to get back to the tower was probably the same as it took to get through the tunnel, but it felt faster.

At the tower they went inside and found everything was exactly as they had left it. They went into the trap door, down the stairs, and into the hallway outside the room with the suits of armour. Brian opened the door and found the suit of armour was in the way, but the others, who were sitting on the floor waiting, heard the door open.

"Good, you got back here," Glenda said, *"We will get rid of the suit of armour in just a moment."* She cast the spell and the suit of armour fell to pieces. Brian stepped over the pieces coming into the room as did Sherry and Todd.

"What happened?" Paul asked.

"The tunnel took us out to a tree in the forest," Sherry answered, *"And we had to walk back to the tower."*

"Well, let us move on," Brian said.

Driscoll stopped. Tarak and Lord Salisbury had fallen asleep, while Wyman was fighting it. Driscoll and Luce got into their bedrolls. Luce listened as everyone else fell asleep, but found himself paying attention to other noises around them for any sign that someone was nearby. There were no noises and eventually Luce dropped off to sleep.

Everyone was scared of this man. He was reportedly the one who killed the princess despite the love they had. The madman who had attacked them had jumped off the castle wall into the ocean beyond and the princess had been found dead in the open area, but he had never been found. The citizens always checked for him before they went out, or came back in and no one went up to the castle where it all happened.

Luce was walked along a narrow walkway with high stone walls on both sides. There were other people going alone with him. They reached an area high on the cliff, but made out of the same stone. Window like places were placed at regular intervals around the area. There was a bloody spot in one corner.

"This where he died." Pointing out one of the windows places. "The prince died here as well, but was never found."

Luce saw a shadow on the wall. It was the prince, but only his shadow was left.

"He is still alive," Luce said pointing to the shadow. Everyone looked.

Luce sat up at the sound of horse's hoofs. He sat up and looked around. The dream left him slightly disoriented, but the sight of a unicorn with a fairy riding on its back through his protection spells was enough to make him wonder if he was really awake. He shook his head a few times and blinked a couple times. He finally accepted that he was awake. At which point he remembered that the fairy's name was Sandra and that she went away with the unicorn a while back.

He glanced around and saw that everyone else was still asleep. Luce looked back at the unicorn, which was getting closer. Finally it stopped a distance away and Sandra flew the rest of the way to Luce.

"You said that I would find you when I was finished," Sandra said.

"So, you have," Luce said after clearing his throat, "Did you succeed in whatever it was that he needed your help with?"

"His name is Harold," Sandra said, "And yes, I did succeed, but I am not supposed to tell you about it. However, because it was so successful that Harold offered to help out the quest. I did not know exactly what you all needed, but I thought maybe that you could use some warm food and drink. Things that humans find cheerful."

"We could use some cheer," Luce said, "Since the forest does not seem to want us here. It keeps having animals attack us. Lord Salisbury has a broken arm and Driscoll several scratches. And then there is whoever is following us."

"Might be able to get a healing potion that will actually work," Sandra said, "But there is nothing he can do about the attacks or being followed."

"Food and drink will help boost the mood," Luce said, "With a more cheerful mood, everything else will be easier."

"Okay," Sandra said. She went back over to where Harold was waiting. They spoke in voices too quiet for Luce to hear them. He looked up at the sky to try and figure out the approximate time. It was getting close to morning, but an hour or more than the usual time they got up. If there was food provided no one would miss much sleep, but Luce was not going to wake them up just yet.

Sandra flew back to him carrying a bottle about as big as she as. He caught it before she dropped it. There was no label, but the liquid was clear and coloured red.

"Harold said you add a mouthful or two to the person's drink and it will heal them without them tasting it," Sandra said.

"Thank you," Luce said to Harold. Harold nodded back.

Find help from beyond, Harold told him. Luce nodded, but really did not know what it meant.

In the meantime, Harold said, *Eat.* To one side of the

camp a table appeared. On the table was everything a person could want for breakfast. At one end of the table was three steaming pitchers even though the air was not that cold.

Luce looked back at Harold to thank him, but the unicorn was gone.

"He had places he needed to go," Sandra said.

"That is okay," Luce said as he got up. He went over to the table and poured five cups from the pitchers, which gave off the smell of mulled cider. Luce poured a little bit of the healing potion into one glass and a mouthful into another glass. Then he put the healing potion away.

Luce went over to the rest of the group.

"Wake up," Luce shook the shoulder of Driscoll first and then quickly moved to the rest. Tarak and Wyman sat up immediately ready for danger, while Driscoll and Lord Salisbury were a little slower.

"What is that?" Driscoll asked looking at the table. They could all smell the food and they wanted to eat, but were hesitant.

"I brought it," Sandra answered from where she had sat down on one of the six chairs that were there.

Luce picked up the two cups he had dosed with healing potion.

"Come on try some," Luce offered the cup with a little to Driscoll and the one with the mouthful to Lord Salisbury. Both took the cups, but Lord Salisbury was hesitant to drink. Luce took two of the remaining cups and offered them to Tarak and Wyman. Tarak took an immediate drink, but Wyman wanted and watched Tarak.

"It is good," Tarak said.

"Feel strange?" Wyman asked.

"I feel warm," Tarak answered, "It tastes delicious." Wyman still waited, but Driscoll drank some of his cider.

"Best I have ever tasted," Driscoll said before heading to the table. Luce was already there and taking a little bit of everything because it all looked good. Driscoll took a little of everything as well. Lord Salisbury and Wyman were still slightly suspicious, but Tarak took a plate of his own before sitting down with Driscoll and Luce.

Finally Lord Salisbury tried his cider and decided he liked it enough to join them in eating. Wyman sat, but did not touch any of the food for several minutes. He was finally convinced to try it when Sandra took some and started eating. She did not take much, but she did not need as much to feel full.

They ate and drank until they were all full. There was still some food left, but it was only small amounts of this and that. Driscoll's scratches had disappeared, but no one had really noticed. Lord Salisbury at some point during the meal found himself in need of both hands and used them without really noticing he did it until it was over, but he did not tell anyone. He did get rid of the sling, but otherwise did not say anything about it. When they were finished eating, Luce and Tarak dumped the food in the bushes and put dirt over them. Then with cheerful tones and uplifted spirits, the group packed up camp, mounted their horses, and continued along the path. The path might have gone on forever, but today that did not matter. They knew that they were going to be attacked by something this afternoon, but that did not matter either. As they went the group laughed and joked. They were aware of the person still following and still watchful.

They stopped for lunch and Luce distributed food out of a basket which had come with the table of food. It had stayed warm in the basket. It was enough for everyone without there being any leftovers. Luce left the basket in the bushes on the side of the path. They still ate while on their horses because there was no other place to sit.

The afternoon went on to the point in time where the invisible line appeared and the animals would attack. They stopped and dismounted. Lord Salisbury took the reins of the horses and took them back from the action. He tied them to a bush before joining the rest for the fight. Everyone pulled out their weapons and got ready to fight. Sandra had spent the day on Luce's shoulder, now she flew on her own. She had used up all her energy dealing with the unicorn's problem, so she had been absorbing the energy from the amulet. Now she had enough she could hold her own in the fight against whatever animal showed up.

Wyman checked to make sure everyone was ready. Once they had all nodded, he moved forward. He went passed the invisible line. Suddenly snakes started coming out of the bushes and falling out of trees. It was all different kind of snakes, some poisonous and some not. Luce and Driscoll recognized which ones were poisonous and were attacking those ones first. Tarak, Wyman, and Lord Salisbury slashed at anything that slithered. Sandra was making the ones she pointed at disappear.

There were plenty of snakes to deal because for every one killed more seemed to show up. That and every snake killed became a slippery spot on the path. They fought, tried to avoid stepping on the corpses, and keep the snakes off themselves. Luce started using his fire spell on the corpses so he could stop slipping. It helped a little as he worked on splitting his attention between slicing through the poisonous snakes and using the spell.

Eventually the amount of snakes decreased. Luce switched to just burning up the dead snakes. Only once the snakes were dealt with did Sandra help him out. When they were finished all that was left were some charred areas on the path. No one had any bites or other injuries. Lord Salisbury went back and got the horses. Everyone mounted and they continued on their journey.

"No wonder you said the forest was not happy with you here," Sandra said, "I have never seen so many snakes in one group before and they were all different varieties, which you would never see together. You have been attacked before?"

"First there were squirrels, then bears, cougars, and crows," Luce answered, "And now snakes. All creatures that reside in this forest and all are apparently plentiful."

"And animals attacking in ways they would not normally attack unless directed to by something else," Sandra said, "I understand why you would say the forest does not want you here. I am not sure there is anything you can do anything about it but keep moving and find a way out here."

"We tried to leave the path," Driscoll said, "We cut our way through the bushes, but only ended up back on the path at the exact spot we started, just on the other side of the path. We have also been going along this path for several days now and there is no end in sight. The yesterday someone started following us, but we cannot see them despite the straightness of the path behind us."

"There is something wrong with this path," Lord Salisbury said.

"The only thing the forest is not likely to do is have someone follow you," Sandra said, "The forest does not need anything to do the watching for it, the forest knows where we are all the time."

"Well, then something has decided to follow us," Luce said, "And we have not been able to see them."

"Well, if they were dangerous I would assume they would have attacked by now," Sandra said, "So, I would worry more about the forest than whatever is following."

"We just need to figure out how to get off this path and get to the portal," Luce said, "I think Harold tried to tell me, but I do not understand it."

"Harold?" Driscoll asked.

"The friend Sandra left us to go help," Luce answered. Driscoll nodded.

"What did he tell you?" Sandra asked.

"'Find help from beyond'," Luce answered.

"He probably means for you to ask the help of a saint," Sandra said.

"I do not look to saints to solve my problems," Luce replied, "I never have and we have not gotten along for it. I will not prostrate myself for any such thing."

"Maybe this is your test from above," Sandra said, "God is known for sending personal tests to bring people back to him."

"I do not care what he has planned," Luce said, "I can follow this path a long time before I feel the need to prostrate before a saint without any guarantee I will get what I need out of the whole thing."

"I do not think this whole adventure will come to that," Driscoll said, "We will leave this forest and this path long before any such thing will be necessary."

"Okay," Sandra said she settled herself in on Luce's shoulder as close to the amulet as possible.

When evening arrived so did the clearing for them to camp in. They had setting up camp down to an easy routine. There was no more food from this morning left, but they still had food they had brought with them, which could be cooked into a good meal. Luce had put up the protection spells once they had stopped so he did not have to do it later. When supper was over, everyone sat back to listen to the next part of the story.

"So, the group turned to the next door with the suit of armour in front of it," Driscoll said,

Paul cast the spell to deal with the suit of armour, but this time the suit of armour did not fall. Paul got ready to cast the spell again, but before he could all the suits of armour came to live and attacked the group. The group fought as best they could and ended up being pushed back out the door that Brian, Sherry, and Todd had come in. When all of them had been pushed through the door was closed.

"Apparently you can only knock down one suit of armour at a time before they attack," Brian said as he opened the door again. All the suits of armour were back in their places.

"Since all it does is reset the room, it is fine," Glenda said, "Let us continue on." They went to the next door. Paul cast the spell and the suit of armour fell apart. None of the rest of the suits of armour moved. Sherry went and checked the door. Once she opened it, the group followed her inside.

What they entered was not a room exactly. Immediately in front of them were two stone walls with a doorway in the middle of it. The walls created a tunnel went down to meet another tunnel going perpendicular to this tunnel. There were lit torches at regular intervals, so it was easy to see things.

"A maze," Paul said, "This should not be too difficult for us."

"Lead away," Brian said.

Paul entered the tunnel and everyone followed him. He stopped at the junction and checked both ways. There were no obvious clues as to which way to go. Paul took an experimental sniff of the air and then checked both ways again.

"This way," He pointed to the right. This tunnel went down to another one that was perpendicular. Paul ignored the right turn and led the group to the left. This tunnel went around another two more lefts before they reached another junction. Paul led them right which went straight for a short while before going right again. This was followed by another right. Straight

down here was an area with small space on the left with a wall in front of them and a right turn into a long straight with went in both directions.

Paul once again stopped to figure which direction to go. He glanced down both hallways several times before going right.

"The other direction will take us back to the beginning," Paul explained to the others. Behind the wall there was another tunnel that went to the right, but Paul ignored it completely. He led the group straight to the end of the tunnel. The only way to turn at that point was left which went to another left. This ended at a junction. The right led to another straight hallway and the left went to another left.

Paul held up his hand to signal for everyone to stay there before venturing down the left tunnel. He looked around the corner and came back toward the group shaking his head.

"This way," Paul pointed to the right. The group followed him into the next hallway. The right direction went straight before ending at a wall. The left direction went to another left turn. Paul headed left. They reached the end and turned left again, which went down another tunnel to another left turn.

They made this turn to end up in a small room with a door in the opposite corner. Sherry took the lead as far as the door. She checked it over and deemed it safe, but when she tried to open it the door would not move.

"We are stuck in here," Sherry said.

"Do we need to go back and find another way?" Glenda asked.

"Or do we have to fight some enemy hiding around

here?" Brian asked.

The torch in the one corner flashed red and then it was back to normal. Everyone looked at it.

"Is it answering us?" Brian asked, "Or is it a signal for the enemies to attack?"

"We will wait a few minutes," Paul said, "If the enemies show up, we will fight them and get out of here. If not we will figure out what is going on."

Everyone got their weapons ready as they waited. After five minutes, they were starting to get restless.

"If it signals for enemies, they are really slow enemies," Paul said. The group looked back at the torch. The red came back briefly and then disappeared again.

"So, not bringing enemies," Brian said, "Then what does it do?"

"Did it blink during the wait?" Glenda asked.

"I do not think so," Paul answered, "But I was not paying attention. Was anyone?" He glanced around and everyone shook their head.

"What else could it be for?" Julie asked. No one answered, but they all waited. Five minutes later the torch blinked again. Sherry was close to the door and she turned toward it at the blink of the torch. She went over and pulled it open.

"Apparently the red light means the door is open," Sherry said turning to the others.

"Then let us get going," Paul said. They followed Sherry through the door and Paul took the lead on the other side. This was a right turn that went to a left turn at the end of the wall. The end of this tunnel was a right turn, which went to a tunnel that went straight for a

while. They reached another right turn, which brought them to another long hallway. The end of this hallway, they rounded the corner to the left which was a tunnel running parallel to the one they had just gone down. At the end of this one was a door. There was no torches blinking red and Sherry checked the door to find it opened easily. The group followed Sherry through it.

And found themselves back at the beginning part of the maze with the tunnel in the middle of the stone walls. On the right side of the wall was red numbers written on it. It read twenty-eight.

"What is that?" Paul asked.

"Our time through the maze, I think," Glenda answered, "To get out of here, we need to decrease the amount of time we are in the maze."

"Let us try again," Brian said as he started down the tunnel. He took the left tunnel instead of the right. This led to a tunnel running perpendicular to the one they were in. Brian led the group right to a tunnel that went straight for a while and stopped at a wall with another tunnel to the right. This one was the long tunnel with two tunnels off it to the right and a third at the very end that went off to the left. Brian took the second tunnel on the right. The group followed him. There was a turn to the right and straight into a small room, where the door closed behind them.

Rather than searching for the way to open the door, or even trying to open the door they waited. Finally one of the torches flashed red and Sherry opened the door. The group trouped out of the small room. They went back to the straight tunnel with the three tunnels off it.

Brian led them into this tunnel and went straight to

the end of the tunnel and around the left turn. The next turn was left, which brought them to a junction. Brian turned to the right and the rest followed. This went into a straight tunnel with a blank wall on one end and a left turn at the other end. The left turn led to another left turn. This brought them back into the room with the red flashing torch. Here they had to wait until the torch flashed and then Brian opened the door. The group followed Brian around the right corner with another right turn. They went along this tunnel to another right turn. This led to the first of two straight tunnels that ended at the door out of the maze. The group stepped through the door.

And stepped back into the beginning of the maze. This time the writing on the wall read fifteen.

"We did it faster," Glenda said.

"We just need to do it faster," Sherry said, "Or that seems to be what needs to be done." She took the lead this time. She went left, right, right, left, left, right, left, left, and into the room where the group had to wait for the light. Once out the door, Sherry led them right, right, right, straight, left around the wall, and straight to the door. She opened it and they all stumbled through. They found themselves back in the room with the suits of armour. They stopped to rest before dealing with any more.

Lord Salisbury was snoring loud enough for Driscoll to stop the story. Tarak and Wyman laid down and closed their eyes. Driscoll and Luce got into their bedrolls. Driscoll was asleep shortly, but Luce found himself lying awake staring up at the sky. He blinked a couple times and the stars moved each time.

He rolled over to try and get some sleep, to find it about the time he usually got up. Luce sat up and looked around. It was the right time of the morning, but he felt like he had not gotten any sleep at all. But he just stretched and got breakfast started.

Everyone else woke up at their usual time and everything else went the same as the usual routine. Soon they were mounted on their horses and continuing along the path. Everyone, except Luce, was cheerful and in a good mood. Luce spent most of the time lost in his own tiredness. Fortunately nothing happened he was needed for.

They ate lunch while riding and in the middle of the afternoon they reached the place when they were usually attacked. Wyman stopped before the invisible line. Only now did Luce start to pay attention to his surroundings. Everyone got ready to fight whatever animal would appear when the line was crossed. Lord Salisbury had tied the horse's reins to a bush far back from the fight.

Wyman checked to make sure that everyone was ready before crossing the invisible line. The moment he did large, brown spiders started to descend on the group. Luce put a protection spell around them before the spiders reached the group. He recognized the spider and knew they were poisonous. The spiders reached the protection spell and showed it for the dome it was. There were so many spiders they could not see the trees above them. The spiders tried to burrow into the protection spell, but they could not do it.

"We are dead if that fails," Lord Salisbury said,

"Those spiders will make short work of us."

"The protection spell will not fail," Luce said, "But we cannot attack with any physical weapons."

"What about the horses?" Lord Salisbury asked. Everyone looked toward them. Between the spiders, they could see the horses standing calmly where they had been left. The spiders appeared to have no interest in anything other than the group.

"They are fine," Driscoll said, "So, if we cannot physically attack them, what can we do?"

"Wait," Luce answered.

Driscoll, Lord Salisbury, and the two guards gathered in a circle a short distance from Luce, but did not put their weapons away.

"How far can you spread the fire?" Luce asked Sandra.

"About twice the size of normal," Sandra answered, "But it will be not as powerful."

"That is fine," Luce said. He cast the fire spell and Sandra manipulated it before the spell reached the target. The fire landed on the spiders at the top of the dome and actually lit the spiders on fire rather than just turn them to ash. The fire spread to other spiders as the ones already on fire bumped into others. Some just gave up and died from the flames, but none of them burned completely to ash.

Luce cast another spell and Sandra manipulated the spell in the same way as the last one. It was slightly to the left of the first spell and different spiders were underneath it. The flames spread to other spiders when they were bumped into. Luce and Sandra continued to do their magic as the spider population decreased. With the amount of spiders, the top of the dome did not clear. Instead the corpses blocked the view.

When all the spiders had stopped moving, Luce used his cleaning spell to remove the spiders from the protection spell and into the bushes on either side. Luce made sure all the spiders were in the bushes, so if there were any alive they would crawl on to the path and be seen so they could be killed. The group sat down and waited within the protection spell. After ten minutes there were no signs of any of the spiders. They waited another five minutes, but still nothing. Finally they decided all the spiders were dead.

Luce dropped the protection spell. They waited another two minutes, but there was still no sign of any of the spiders. Lord Salisbury brought the horses back to the group and they remounted. The group got moving along the path.

When they reached the clearing for the night, the group stopped and made up camp. Luce helped Tarak make supper and Wyman cleaned up afterward. When everything was finished they all sat around the fire and waited for Driscoll to start to story for the evening.

"The group got ready to move on to the next door," Driscoll started,

Everyone, except Sherry who remained seated, packed up everything they had taken out and got to their feet. The group were just about to head to the door, when they realized Sherry had not moved.

"What is wrong?" Glenda asked.

"A headache with flashing lights," Sherry answered, "And severe cravings for cookies."

"*It is the habituopiate,*" *Paul said,* "*Those are the beginning symptoms. She needs more antidote.*"

"*I have something stronger,*" *Glenda said digging into her bag,* "*It should deal with any lingering effects.*" *She found the bottle and offered it to Sherry, who took a drink. Sherry offered it back.*

"*Take another drink,*" *Glenda said. Sherry did so, only then did Glenda accept the bottle back.*

"*If you find yourself suffering from any other symptoms then ask for some more of it,*" *Glenda said.*

"*I will,*" *Sherry said,* "*I am starting to feel better already. Give me another minute.*"

The group waited. Sherry took a little bit of time and then she got up. Finally she was ready to go on. They got ready with Brian, Sherry, and Todd at the front and Paul, Glenda, and Julie at the back. They moved toward the final door in the room. Paul cast the spell and the suit of armour collapsed. Sherry stepped around the pieces and checked the door.

She jumped back before there was a lightning arc. Glenda stepped forward, but stopped when Sherry held up her hand. Glenda stepped back to the rest of the group. Sherry went back to the door. She worked on it for several minutes before trying to open it. The door opened without anything happening.

Sherry stepped back and let Brian go through first. Everyone else followed. This room was long with numerous tables full of laboratory equipment. Painted at various spots on the floor around the room were circles and symbols. At the far end of the room was a large wooden door with a stone golem standing in front of it. The golem did not move and gave no indication it was animated.

"The wizard and Lady Erica's niece must be through that door," Paul said, "We just need to deal with the golem."

"And what is the best method of doing that?" Brian asked, "Straight attacking, magic, or a combination of the two."

"Likely a combination of the two," Paul answered, "But be careful of everything in this room, especially your footing." Everyone nodded before starting forward.

The golem did not move as the group got closer. There were three circles painted on the floor around the golem, one in front and one on each side of it. The door was behind it. Everyone was careful of the circles, but despite being so close the golem did not move. Brian poked the golem with the top of his axe and it still did not move.

"What is going on with it?" Julie asked.

"It is not animated at the moment," Brian answered, "But I would guess something has to happen for us to trigger it."

"That would be the circles," Paul said, "From the looks of it. Perhaps if we are all careful, we can get through the door without having to fight the golem."

"Let us see about this door then," Sherry said as she carefully moved behind the golem. She avoided the circles. She carefully checked over the door. After a minute she took out her lock pick and unlocked the door. Sherry gently pushed it open a little bit and peeked inside.

"What is in there?" Brian asked.

"*The wizard's bedroom,*" *Sherry answered quietly,* "*And he seems to be asleep.*"

"*Maybe we can get him by surprise,*" *Glenda said,* "*If he does not have a chance to fight, we are less likely to get hurt.*"

"*Let us go,*" *Brian said. He avoided the circles and went up against the wall. He shuffled along the wall to the door. Sherry stepped into the room and Brian followed her through. Todd had an easier time slipping behind the golem and through the door. Glenda went next. She did similar to Brian and carefully made her way passed the golem. Once she was in the room, Julie moved around the circles and the golem into the room.*

Paul made sure she was through before starting toward the door himself. He stepped around the circle on the left side of the golem and was about to slip passed it. Paul misstepped and he fell to one knee. His foot ended up in the circle. Golem's eyes light up and it turned to Paul. He barely managed to fall back and out of the golem's reach before the stone hand could grab him. Paul peddled backward away from the golem, which turned toward him. The door behind the golem closed and made the sound of it locking.

Paul got far enough away he felt safe enough to get up and run. The golem followed him at a slower pace. Paul was careful of the circles on the floor as he headed toward the nearest table. He got behind it and looked back at the golem. The golem was still headed his direction, but Paul could easily outrun it. He looked around, but there was not much he could use to defend against the golem. Paul thought about it for a minute, but the golem was just about to the table. An idea came to him and Paul quickly cast the spell. He had just finished when the golem reached the table and smashed his fist through it. The table folded inward and caused all the things on it to pile into the middle. The golem brushed aside the debris.

The spell created a shadow double of Paul, which looked exactly like him. The double appeared right next to Paul. Before the golem could reach Paul, he ran one way and his double ran the other. The golem looked after both of them and then headed after the shadow double. Paul had gone around the pieces of the table in the direction of the door and headed straight for it. He tried to open it, but it would not open as much as he tried.

The golem continued to chase after Paul's double and destroyed anything that got in its way. Paul turned back to the laboratory. He noticed the golem, despite not paying attention to its feet, was not stepping in the circles painted on the floor. He tried the door again, but it was stuck and would not open.

The golem smashed through another table when the spell ran out and Paul's shadow double disappeared. The golem looked around for its target. Paul went to the side of the room to have tables between him and the golem. His foot half entered the circle near the door, which caused the golem to turn toward him. Paul went the rest of the way and crouched down in hopes the golem would miss him behind the table. From there he watched at the golem headed right for him. Just as Paul was thinking up a different spell to try, the golem's foot went into one of the circles. There was a loud bang and the stone golem became flying bits of rock. Paul found himself covering his head to avoid the debris. It took a few minutes before it was finished raining pieces.

When it was done, Paul got to his feet and dusted himself off. The golem was definitely gone. Paul went to the door and tried to open it again. It took a few shoves with his shoulder, but eventually opened.

When the door had closed behind Julie, everyone had turned at the sound. Julie tried to open it back up, but it would not move. Sherry went over and did a check of the door while everyone else looked around the room. It was not as long as the last room, but it seemed to be in two halves. The one closest to the door was empty and the far end had a bed, a chest, and a table. There was also a cage to one side in which sat a girl, who could not have been anyone other than Lady Erica's niece. Dawn had seen them, but still looked worried. The wizard was lying in the bed and was asleep. Shortly after the door had closed, he smiled and rolled over.

Once Sherry was sure that there was no way to open the door, she rejoined everyone in surveying the room. No one wanted to talk for fear of waking the wizard. Todd and Brian moved forward, but a few feet from the bedroom set up they found an invisible wall that would not let them go any farther. They checked it all the way across, but could not find any way around the thing. Glenda and Julie worked with the magic as much as they could, but could not cause it to come down. Working as quietly as they could the whole group tried to figure out a way through the invisible wall and still not wake the wizard. It seemed impossible.

There was a large bang from the previous room and the wizard sat straight up in bed. The group froze in place. The wizard looked at them, but did not say anything. He got out of bed and started chanting that included arm waving. Everyone backed toward the door.

At that moment, Paul managed to break through the door and looked around the room. He recognized the spell and rushed into the room to shout the counter spell in time to stop whatever effect from taking hold of the group.

"There is a shield between him and us," Glenda said, "Something powerful and not easily disabled."

"I will try," Paul said. He started to throw spells that would take it down between countering spells from the wizard. Brian went close to the invisible wall and poked at it after every one of Paul's spells.

Finally the axe went through where it had not before. As soon as that happened, Brian headed for the wizard. Paul kept the wizard busy, while the rest of the group rushed in to attack. The wizard did what he could defend his person while still dealing with the spells from Paul. He worked hard at it and managed to avoid getting hit, but his power weakened as the battle progressed.

The battle ended when he collapsed from exhaustion. He no longer had any power to cast spells, or defend himself. Everyone stopped attacking and backed off. Sherry went to the cage, where Dawn was now standing and leaning against the bars.

"Is he dead?" Dawn asked staring at the fallen

wizard.

"Not yet," Sherry answered, "But he might as well be." Sherry worked on the lock for a minute before the cage door opened and Dawn was able to step out.

"Let us put him inside before we leave," Glenda said.

"That is a good idea," Julie said.

The wizard was placed inside the cage and Sherry locked the door behind him. Julie sung a spell that made sure there was a shield around the cage which would not let magic be cast by the person inside or out. Unless the wizard was good at lock picking he would be stuck in the cage for a very long time.

The group made sure they had everything and then took Dawn out of the tower. They closed all of it up behind them and made sure the basement of the tower was not easily accessed by any ordinary person. Then they went back through the forest. They did not encounter any resistance on their way. Once they reached the field, it was a short walk back to Lady Erica's manor house.

Lady Erica welcomed them back and was very grateful to have her niece back. She offered them supper, which they accepted. When that was over, she paid them well for their work and let them have a ride back to town. Everyone headed for the tavern to have a few drinks before going to their rooms for the night.

The next morning everyone went off. Sherry and Todd were headed off to the temple of Meslow. Paul and Brian headed off together because they were going to roughly the same direction. Glenda was headed back to her own garden since a message had reached the town that Lauren had to leave and Glenda wanted to get there before her plants were troubled. Julie headed off to find a tavern who could use a bard for a short time and was willing to pay good coin, or serve good meals.

Everyone was still wake, but with the end of the story they all got into their bedrolls. Lord Salisbury and Driscoll were the first to drop off with Tarak and Wyman not far behind. Luce fought sleep for a few more minutes, but ended up giving in because he could not think of any reason to stay awake.

There was a troll. Ten feet, green, hair in the wrong places, and a large wooden club it was swinging around. Luce found himself in a maze like area and he was running away from the troll. He would run along one passage way without a top, but the troll would hit it with its club and cave in part of the passage way so Luce could not go that way. Luce would head down another passage way, but the troll's club would come down and the way would be blocked. Luce tried another passage way to have the same thing happen. He tried to cast a spell on the troll, but found it only made the troll bigger and swing farther.

Luce tried to run faster, but he could not seem to out run the troll. He stumbled through a doorway and found himself in a forest being chased by a hellcat. He could not use his magic and it was gaining on him with every step his took to get away. He could not stop and fight it because he was too small to swing his sword. Luce tripped and fell down on the path getting himself all dirty. Tears poured down his face as he turned to look at the hellcat. The hellcat stopped and got ready to pounce, but before it did it became a man standing over Luce with a sword in his hand ready to strike. Luce pulled his own out and got ready to bring it up to defend himself.

Luce sat up and looked around. It appeared to be about the usual time he woke up, but something had to have woken him. He listened carefully, but there were no noises or people to disturb his sleep. He sat for several more minutes, but there was nothing. Luce shook himself out of it and started breakfast.

The rest of the group slowly woke up as usual and the morning went along the routine that was normal for them. They ate breakfast, cleaned up from breakfast, packed up, and then mounted their horses. They could still feel someone following them as they started along the path, but they could not see who the person was. The cheerfulness of the last couple days was starting to wear off and all but two were back to wondering why they were wandering along a path with no end. Driscoll tried, briefly, to get the cheerful mood back early in the day, but the only person willing to go along with it was Luce.

Lunch was eaten as they rode because there was no real point in stopping. The path offered no place to stop and the forest was close tightly around the path to stop any thoughts aside from forward. Forward did not seem to hold any more answers than the path behind them did. They just knew they could not go right or left.

Afternoon came with the usual sense there was

something ahead, which would be on the other side of an invisible line in the path and force them to fight against some creature of the forest. Luce figured it had to be a non-magical, because the magical ones appeared to be able to avoid being caught it the forest's magic. Everything they had fought so far were normal forest creatures. However, when they reached and stopped where they were usually attacked, they found a pile of ashes in the middle of the path.

"The squirrels," Driscoll said, "That is exactly as we had left the squirrels."

"It is," Luce answered, "It appears we have been going around a loop."

"How can we?" Lord Salisbury asked, "We have been going straight along this path."

"The magic of the forest can do many things," Luce said, "Since the forest has been attacking us, I would say the looping is also a way for the forest to get rid of trespassers. It sends people around the loop and attack them until they died in the fights or run out of supplies."

"This cannot have been the way my grandfather went to the portal," Driscoll said, "In all the stories I heard, there was nothing about the magical abilities of the forest, or a looping path. We must have entered the forest at a different place than he had gone."

"Maybe he went along the road and entered that direction," Luce said.

"Which is fine for him," Lord Salisbury said, "But what are we to do? We are currently stuck along a loop in a forest that is not happy to have us here and is trying to kill us."

"Ask for help," Driscoll answered, "All travellers who get lost have the option of asking for help from Saint Nitesh. He will send directions out and we will be able to continue our quest to find the portal."

"So, what do we have to do?" Lord Salisbury asked.

"Get down from the horses and ask for his help," Driscoll answered.

Everyone got down from their horses and gathered in a circle. Luce took the time to have a drink. Driscoll went down on his knees.

"Saint Nitesh," Driscoll said, "Travellers are in need of your help. We are lost in an enchanted forest and wish for help breaking out of the enchantment. For in our state we cannot find our way."

The path melted away and the group found themselves in a fairly dense area of trees. However, they could see in all directions. It looked like an ordinary forest and all the sounds of an ordinary forest could be heard. The noise was no longer muffled. There was still no sign of which direction they should go.

"We search for a specific thing," Driscoll continued, "A portal from which magic used to flow. We wish for something to show us the way and get us out of this place. Do what you can and do what you will. We shall wait for your choice and hopeful you are merciful to the lost traveller."

LUCE REACHES HIS QUEST END AND DRISCOLL MEETS HIS AUNT, BUT THEY BRING ALONG SOMETHING THEY DID NOT MEAN TO

Driscoll had barely finished uttering the words when a white wolf stepped out from behind a far off tree. Luce stared at it in wonder and awe. It looked back at him with bright blue eyes.

"A wolf!" Tarak cried, "Shoot it before it attacks is."

"Don't!" Luce shouted grabbing Wyman's arm before he could take out his bow. Wyman stared at Luce like he was crazy.

"It will attack us," Tarak said.

"No, it will not," Luce replied, "It is our answer to prayer. It will lead us to the portal, all we have to do is follow it."

Luce had let go of Wyman and was gathering up his stuff. Driscoll had scrambled to his feet and getting his gear. Luce and Driscoll headed toward the wolf leaving the other three to hurry and follow them.

The branches seemed to reach out and grab at them. At time the wolf disappeared behind a tree and they had to search to keep it in sight. They had completely forgotten their horses and were running on foot. The trees were still thick and the way was not smooth, but they hurried along. There was a fear in them that if they did not hurry they would lose the white wolf and never be able to leave this forest or find the portal. Bushes seemed to reach out to trip them up and the forest still felt like it was against them. Neither Driscoll or Luce let the forest slow them down. They knew where they needed to go and nothing was going to get between them and their destination.

They reached a clearing that did not look natural. It looked dead. The white wolf stopped in the middle of the clearing. Luce and Driscoll stumbled into the clearing and saw the white wolf, who turned to look at them. Then the white wolf disappeared.

The noise of Tarak and Wyman stumbling into the clearing caused Driscoll and Luce to look back. Lord Salisbury followed the guards. The three of them had enough sense to bring the horses with them, though it was quite obvious it would be impossible to ride the horses with the density of the forest outside the clearing and the horses had not really liked coming this far into the forest. Lord Salisbury left them at the edge of the clearing.

"What now?" Lord Salisbury asked Driscoll and Luce, "It looks like your white wolf has led you to a dead end."

"It is not a dead end," Luce said, "Look around at this clearing. It is an exact circle. The forest around it is alive, but this space is dead. The sky is different here than it was before we stepped into the clearing. We must be at the clearing where the portal is."

"But where is the portal then?" Driscoll asked, "From the stories I expected it to be here."

"This must be what happened to the magic," Luce said, "Someone closed the portal which cut off the magic to the whole region. Any magic left is either residual, or coming from another portal."

"There are more portals?" Lord Salisbury asked, "Then why did you have to come find this one?"

"If the portal is shut, what can we do?" Driscoll asked.

"I do not know," Luce answered, "I had hoped to talk with the portal guardian and get answers, but if the portal is closed I have some of my answers."

"The portal can never be completely closed," Sandra said, "The portal guardian can close off the worlds from each other, but the portal guardian can still open them back up."

"But how do we communicate with the portal guardian?" Driscoll asked.

"I do not know," Sandra answered, "But I need to get through the portal and back to my home, so there must be some way of getting through."

"Maybe if we call out to the portal guardian," Driscoll suggested, "It worked to talk to the saint, maybe the portal guardian is similar."

"We can try it," Luce said with a shrug. Driscoll nodded and prepared himself to call.

Nastaran came back into her body and quickly got to her feet. They were here! And she just needed to get them through the portal. She hurried out of her room and rushed down the grand staircase. Nastaran left the hut and went over to the three wells. She looked into the one that went to her mother's world. It showed the image of five men standing in a clearing. Nastaran looked deeper and saw the fairy as well. She smiled and giggled.

Nastaran turned and went back into the hut. She went up the grand staircase and went along the left hallway to the library. She stopped outside the doorway. Nastaran straightened her posture and dusted off her clothes as well as smoothing her hair. Only once that was all finished did she step into the library. Her mother was sitting there in discussion with her old friend Parisa. They had been talking all morning about what was going on in Parisa's world.

"Mother," Nastaran said.

Nava looked up at her. Parisa took a sip of tea before doing the same.

"Yes?" Nava's voice suggested that this interruption was unnecessary.

"There are people in the clearing looking for the portal," Nastaran said.

"I know," Nava replied, "But their presence does not mean I should let them through the portal. Many people have wandered into the clearing and I have not brought them through. In fact I sealed that side of the portal so people could not go through it. They can find the portal closed and move along."

"There is a fairy among them," Nastaran said, "She does not belong in that world. She probably got lost and wants to go home."

"Nastaran," Nava's voice held the usual irritation of a mother tired of explaining things to her child.

"This is the group that is destined to stop the madman," Nastaran said, "The one who is undefeatable by everything you have already sent to deal with him."

"You cannot know that," Nava said.

"Yes, I can," Nastaran said, "The Reeze told me and the Saint Nitesh sent for me to guide them to the portal. They are destined to be here and destined to fight the madman."

"You can talk to them and see if they are willing to try," Parisa said, "You should at least let the fairy through."

"All right, I will talk to them," Nava said, "But I do not really expect them to be what is needed to defeat the madman." Nava got to her feet. Nastaran did not say anything else as she followed her mother out of the library. They went down the staircase and out of the hut. Her mother went over to the wells. She looked into the one and nodded in confirmation.

"Portal guardian, please hear us and come speak with us," Driscoll directed his comments to the air in the middle of the clearing. The group waited for a mere minute before two women appeared in the centre of the clearing. The one in the front was probably in her thirties. She had long, brown hair braided back out of her face. She was about five feet in height and looked like she was good in a fight, despite not having any weapons on her. She wore a sapphire gown and a silver pendent around her neck that glowed slightly. The woman behind was likely in her early twenties. She wore a blue dress matching her eyes, which looked exactly like the white wolf's eyes. Her long, white hair was felt loose around her. She wore no jewellery.

"I am Nava, the portal guardian," the woman in front said, "What do you want?"

"Nava?" Driscoll looked confused, "As in Proster's youngest daughter, Narda."

"A long time ago," the woman confirmed.

"I am of the royal line," Driscoll said, "My father was Zebulon."

"Is he still alive?" Nava asked, "I have heard nothing since I closed the portal."

"No, he died years ago," Driscoll answered, "I have been king since then and currently my son is on the throne until I get back. The kingdom has been doing well."

"What happened to Hertha?" Nava asked.

"She married a noble from Grackle and last anyone heard from them he had been given a position at the great library," Driscoll answered, "They have twins."

"If he was from Grackle, it must have been love," Nava said, "My father would not have accepted such a matching otherwise. I am glad she found love. Now, what is it you want?"

"I started this journey," Luce said, "I have been trying to figure out what happened to the magic and I thought maybe it had something to do with the portal. Since we found it closed, I realized that because the portal was closed it was the reason for the disappearance of the magic. So, the only thing left was to help Sandra return home."

"Good day, Guardian," Sandra said with a bow.

"Good day, fairy," Nava said, "You are most

welcome back through the portal."

"I cannot wait to get home," Sandra said, "It has been a very long time I have seen the home nest."

Driscoll looked like he wanted to ask to see inside the portal and have at least a glimpse of this strange land, but he also remembered his promise to go back to his kingdom and his son.

"I can send you there," Nava said, "But I have a request for this group. Would you like to help them, or just go home?"

"The nest can wait if you think this request will benefit from the help of a fairy," Sandra said.

"I believe all groups benefit from the company of a fairy," Nava said with a smile. Sandra curtsied and then went back to sitting on Luce's shoulder.

"You need our help?" Luce asked.

"We have found we have a problem, which so far none has been able to deal with," Nava answered, "A man showed up one day and no one knows where he is from or how he came here. Those who have met him describe him as a madman. At first no one worried about him, other than to avoid him. However, he had set himself up in a city and the residents had no choice but to flee. His power does not change, but his area of power is growing and those who get in the way are forced to move, or end up dead. Those who have been sent in to deal with him have either not come back or died shortly after arriving back from wounds they received from the madman. There is nothing within my power I can do to get rid of him. I request your group's help in getting rid of this madman from this world."

Driscoll looked at Luce and then to his own men. Tarak and Wyman wanted to go home, but the idea of leaving someone who was in need of their help was wrong. Lord Salisbury knew his king was not going to refuse a chance to see this world which fascinated him for so long and where his king went he would follow. Luce nodded to show he was ready to fight this madman. Sandra just settled in for the ride.

"We will go and see what we can do about this madman," Driscoll said.

"Good," Nava said, "Your horses will have to stay here, but I very much doubt they will wander away. Horses rarely leave the clearing without their owners."

"Then we are ready," Driscoll said.

"Very well," Nava said.

Suddenly the whole group was standing in a field of tall grass. There were mountains in the far distance and trees closer, but mostly it was a large field. The group looked around themselves for a few minutes before turning back to Nava.

"Magic not only works here, but is to most creatures as air is," Nava said, "You will meet creatures that are fairy tales and legends and they will be as normal here as bears and deer are in the other world. I ask you do not hunt while you are here. I am sending my daughter, Nastaran, with you to show you the way." Nava gestured to the younger woman behind her.

"She knows the way," Nava said, "She can also help you with any problems with the locals. And she has magic abilities will help you reach the madman's territory much faster than you can walk. If you have any questions she can answer them. This is the world where she has spent the most time, so there are some things she may not be able to understand from your world. Overall, her presence should make it much easier for you to reach your destination. However, once you reach the boundary of the madman's territory she cannot go any farther with you."

"We appreciate all the help offered," Driscoll said.

"Good luck," Nava said and then she disappeared.

The group stood there for half a minute staring at the space she had just been before their attention shifted to Nastaran.

"You are the white wolf," Driscoll said.

"I am," Nastaran replied, "It is the only shape I can wander your world in. That is the shape my soul takes on when I go out with it."

"My father saw a white wolf on several occasions," Driscoll said, "Were you the same wolf?"

"I was," Nastaran answered.

"But that was years ago," Lord Salisbury said, "Long before King Driscoll was even born."

"I am called ageless by my father's people," Nastaran said, "I am still a child among them. Even to your eyes, I am young. My mother's own aging has slowed since she was made portal guardian and some of that magic affects me. My body is responsible for the rest as it ages at the rate of elves, not humans or dwarves."

"But why would an elf and a mix of human and dwarf have a child?" Luce asked.

"Love," Nastaran answered, "That is my parent's answer to the question. I believe it may be destiny."

"Perhaps we should get going," Lord Salisbury said, "Because the sooner we get there the sooner this whole thing will be over with."

"Of course," Nastaran said, "This way." She headed off to the north east and the group followed her.

The forest looked a long way off, but within half an hour they had reached the edge of the trees. There was a path, which looked like a nice walk. Walking in the field had been hot because the sun was over head and baking everything on the ground. Now with tree branches overhead it was cooler and the slight breeze made them feel refreshed. This path was not straight and things could be seen on either side, but there was nothing of interest and no really good places to stop. Any place looking really good and practically called to the group had a circle of mushrooms which stopped them from being really tempted. They did not need the warning to avoid the circles, they had all been read the fairy tales.

The walk through the forest took a full hour, but it seemed to go fast. On the other side was a valley before a mountainous area. Nastaran started down a narrow hunting trail into the valley, which had enough trees it was impossible to see the bottom. The rest of the group followed her down.

There were some steep spots and a few rough ones, but otherwise the group had no issues getting to the bottom. It took them a little under an hour to get there. At the bottom of the valley was a fairly large river. It was a couple meters across and looked deep. The group stopped for a drink.

"We have not gone very far and I feel like I am thirsty enough to have walked for days," Lord Salisbury said as he filled his water skin in the river.

"The amount of ground we have just gone over would usually take a day or two," Nastaran said, "But I have been using my abilities so we can cover more ground in as short a time as possible. That is what my mother meant when she said I had abilities to get you there faster than you can walk. We should reach the madman's territory in only a couple of hours."

"Is thirst and tiredness effects from the magic?" Luce asked as he refilled his water skin from river.

"Some people end up with those effects, yes," Nastaran answered, "We can rest for a while if you need."

"I would appreciate it," Driscoll said, "I am feeling like I am aging faster than I can walk."

Everyone sat down with the refilled water skins and a little bit of food. Nastaran sat down on a nearby tree stump and waited. Apparently she did not suffer any effects from her magic. It took ten minutes before anyone felt like they had the energy to talk.

"How are we getting across the river?" Lord Salisbury asked, "I do not see the bridge."

"My ability means all serious obstacles are easily passed by or overcome," Nastaran said, "Do not worry about."

Lord Salisbury nodded, but it was obvious he was worried about it.

"Why does your mother think we can do something about the madman when no one else has been able to?" Luce asked.

"I told her," Nastaran answered.

"And how do you know?" Luce asked.

"Because the Reeze told me you were destined to do it," Nastaran answered.

"What is the Reeze?" Driscoll asked.

"He is an assassin," Nastaran answered, "He is really good at his job, but he also spends his off time studying the books of prophecy. There are so many things in those books. It is not just the big things that are predicted, but the small ones as well."

"I see," Luce said, "And does it say how we are supposed to get rid of this madman?"

"No," Nastaran answered, "But you will find the way. I believe in you."

"Thank you," Driscoll said before exchanging a glance with Luce. There was a slight rumbling sound, but the ground did not move. The group glanced around to see what was making the sound, but Nastaran just pulled a crystal ball out of her pocket.

"It is just my mother with a message for me," Nastaran said. The group settled back down. Nastaran said something none of the group understood and the ball cleared. The face of Nava appeared.

"We have made very good time," Nastaran said.

"Good," Nava said, "Because I think the situation just got worse."

"What happened?" Nastaran asked.

"Some other people came through the portal with the group," Nava answered, "I did not notice them for some reason and brought them along. Once you had left, the second group used some sort of magic device to teleport from the field directly into the city the madman has taken over. There was no fighting observed, so we believe the group are helpers or friends of the madman. The guess is two, but that is not known for sure."

"I am sure they will be careful entering the city," Nastaran said, "They have heard the message."

"Whoever the group is, they are dangerous if they can hide so well from natural magic," Nava said, "Especially since they were not seen either. And it is likely the group heard my request for help along with the plan so far. They should be extra careful."

"I will tell them," Nastaran said. The crystal ball went muddy again and Nava's face disappeared. Nastaran put the crystal ball away.

"You all heard that?" Nastaran asked.

"Yes, we did," Driscoll answered.

"Could this group have been the people following us in the forest?" Lord Salisbury asked, "Could they have followed us across the portal to this place?"

"It seems very likely," Luce answered, "If they have magic strong at hiding and disguising themselves it would make sense as to why we never saw them."

"But it also means we let them through," Driscoll said.

"Maybe they are not as powerful as we think," Luce said, "They were not following us for the first part of the loop in the forest. What if it was because it was only at that point they caught up with us? Maybe they were lost in the forest before we arrived and we led them out?"

"That sounds likely," Driscoll said, "But it still means we led them in here and now we should make sure they do not stay. Especially since they know the madman, or they would not have known where to go."

"Then we should get moving," Luce said. Everyone nodded and they started packing up. They all refilled their water skins before turning to Nastaran to say they were ready. She took the lead again and started toward the water. The group followed. When the water splashed up to their ankles, it was hard not to back out, but that did not last very long before they were back on solid ground and their boots were drying out as they walked.

The mountain seemed to be a much easier climb as they went up it and then back down the other side. This took them two hours to do and they stopped briefly a stream on the other side to have a drink and rest for five minutes. After the brief rest they got to their feet again and continued to follow Nastaran.

The journey took them over a few more mountain peaks and through another forest, field, and rocky area. They finally reached the edge of a forest, where Nastaran stopped. Everyone stopped behind her. She turned to the group.

"This is as far as I can go," Nastaran said, "Everything beyond this is the madman's territory. Be careful and you may want to stop to gather your strength before going on."

"Thank you for getting us this far," Driscoll said.

"You are welcome," Nastaran said, "I hope to see you all again when you are done." She shape shifted into a white wolf and was gone before any of the group could say anything more. They were quiet for a minute.

"So, camp here?" Luce asked.

"A little off the path maybe," Driscoll said pointing to the right of where they were standing, "No need to be that easy to pick off."

Everyone worked to set up camp, but they did not unpack too much in case their rest was disturbed. Luce had put up his protection spell, but was very careful of keeping it out of the madman's territory. They ate a supper of cold rations and water before wrapping themselves in their bedrolls and trying to sleep.

Sunlight woke Luce up. He got into a sitting position and looked around. There was something weird about the morning, but he could not quite figure out what it was. Then he realized half the sun was blocked out. He checked the boundaries and found the madman's territory had crept farther out. Their camp was half in it and half out of it.

Tarak and Wyman were waking up as well. It did not take long before they realized the same thing. Luce helped them wake the other two. They packed up the camp in a hurry. They sat down away from the madman's territory to eat more cold rations. They sat there and watched the territory increase at the rate of five centimeters an hour.

When they were finished, the group made sure they had everything before going back to the path. Tarak took the lead and Wyman took the rear. The group started along the path. The forest looked similar to all the others they had seen and passed through since going through the portal, but this one felt different. It was silent, with no birds or other creatures making noise. It felt like the whole forest was dead, the trees just had not dried up yet. The group stayed in the middle of the path and avoided touching any of the plants as if the condition might be contagious. The journey through the forest seemed to last forever.

Finally they stumbled out of the forest to find themselves in a field. All the grass was dead and there was a dark haze in the air that blocked out the sun. The haze also made it difficult to breathe. Everyone found something they could put over their mouth and nose while still being able to breathe. At the far end of the field was a high wall which surrounded the city. The gates of the city were no longer used for keeping anything out. They were rotted wood, one hanging by a hinge and the other lying on the ground. The only thing that could be seen above the wall was a cathedral with tall windows that gave off red light.

"Do you believe this is destiny as predicted by an assassin?" Luce asked Driscoll as they stared across the field into what looked like their doom.

"No," Driscoll answered, "But I do believe we cannot turn back now we have agreed to do what we can to help."

"We may never make it back from there," Luce said.

"Are you scared of death?" Driscoll asked.

"Petrified," Luce answered, "I have lived longer than a man should and I have never made my peace with God."

"Would you like to stop and do so now?" Driscoll asked.

"No," Luce answered, "I had hoped I would never have to do it any time in the near future. However, I cannot turn down the request given to us and I cannot run away when we are so close."

"Then work hard not to die," Driscoll clapped Luce on the shoulder and took the lead. Luce followed him and the rest trailed behind.

The walk across the field was long, but silent. There was nothing alive out here to make any noise. The path was dirt and their footfalls make little to no noise, making it more eerie. The group headed right for the city gates. They stepped over the debris around the gates and stepped into the city itself. There they stopped and looked around.

The sun was a red circle in the haze which hung over the city and provided the main source of light. The city looked like it had been vacant for a long time. The buildings were ruins and looked like no one could live in them. The cobblestones of the streets were chipped, broken, and in a few cases missing entirely. There was a layer of soot on everything making it all appear grungy and unpleasant. The cathedral stood tall, and although it was dirty, nothing was broken on it. The top windows had red light coming from them, but the rest of the windows were dark. The worst part of it all were the crows. They were dark, rough looking, and had glowing red eyes. They circled in the air. They sat on high points through the city. And their cawing was the only sound in the whole place.

The group stood frozen as they looked around. The feeling of everything being dead was strong and the darkness made them all want to turn back. The only thing giving the group hope was the lack of bones. There was none to be seen despite the number of people sent here to deal with the madman. With that thought the group started forward with their weapons out.

The crows left them alone, but watched every movement. They were careful stepping over things and around things. Finally they reached the door to the cathedral. It was a heavy wooden double door with metal accents. It took both Tarak and Wyman pushing to open it enough for the group to step inside. The inside was as dark and dirty as the outside. The windows did not let in any light, so Tarak and Wyman dug out torches and lit them. The light from the torches barely lit up enough space for the group to see what was within a few feet of them and left the rest of the room in darkness. This first room was fairly large from the guess of both torches being several feet apart and there not being any walls in sight. The group moved forward mostly blind.

They stumbled upon the stairs and moved up slowly. They went up for a while and barely saved themselves from falling at the last stair. At the top they went to the right. The light from the torches showed windows, but no light coming through them. The group went along for a long while without finding anything that could give them a sense of where they were or where they should have been going. They could not see any doors off. The only things there appeared to be were bare walls, which gave no indication that would help them.

They reached a dead end. It was a bare wall with no sign of a door. Driscoll and Lord Salisbury searched it for anything, but did not find it. The group turned around and went back toward the stairs, or at least they hoped they were. They stumbled through the dark for a while. Driscoll was just about to take a step when Luce grabbed his arm and pulled him back.

"What?" Driscoll asked.

"Stairs," Luce answered pointing down. Driscoll looked down and barely saw the stairs he was just about fall down. He stepped back, as did everyone else.

"Thank you," Driscoll said.

"Let us just hurry and get through this," Luce said, "Every minute we are in here, we are in more danger. I can feel it in my gut."

"I believe we need to get through here fast, as well," Tarak said.

"The only thing to do is go the other direction," Driscoll said, "Is there anything else we use for light?"

"I have a spell," Luce said, "But I do not know if it will help any more than the torches."

"Might as well try it," Driscoll said, "Maybe it will

show us more than the torches are."

"Okay," Luce said. He took a moment to bring the spell to his mind and then repeated the words. A ball of light appeared above him, but it only gave a little more light than the torches. It was enough they could see the stairs to be able to avoid them, but it did not show much to the left side of the stairs. It followed Luce as they started down the hallway.

There was nothing but bare walls down this hallway. They reached another dead end, which was again searched for secret doors and such. There was nothing there.

"They have to be here somewhere," Driscoll said.

"Maybe there is a door on the other side of the stairs," Wyman said.

"Let us go back and see," Driscoll said.

The group headed back toward the stairs. They avoided stumbling on the stairs because of Luce's ball of light showing it to them in just time. They went around the railing to the other side of the stairs and found another staircase that went upwards. Tarak took the lead and everyone else followed. This was a narrower staircase which curved around to the other direction by the time they reached the top. It was still dark up on this level, but the area was small with two grand doors in the middle. The group started toward the door of the room.

Luce found himself stopping just a few steps from the staircase. The amulet of Saint Onan started feeling so heavy Luce found himself dropping to the floor on to his hands and knees. Everyone else stopped and looked back, but Luce did not notice. He felt like he was choking, but the amulet was not tightening on his neck.

He could still breathe, but it did not feel like it.

Find help from beyond, Harold the unicorn's voice repeated in Luce's head. Luce fought whatever magic was attacking him, but it was a different type magic that he could not fight.

Only help is from beyond, this voice was deeper than Harold's voice and it was one Luce had heard before in certain dreams, *Let me in and get your help.*

Luce fought harder as he always did in his dreams, but he felt like he could not defeat it. There was a bright light glowing in front of him and Luce looked up. Standing over was a large, human like being. It had a large build with muscular arms and a long flowing white robe. There were white eagle wings on its back showing over both shoulders. Most of the light came from a circle above the person's head.

Let go of your fear and accept what you know is truth, the deep voice seem to come from the being, but the mouth did not move. Luce bowed his head to avoid looking at the being and its brightness. The amulet still felt heavy around his neck, but it had stopped choking him.

"I accept this help from beyond," Luce whispered.

You will someday accept the rest, the deep voice responded, *Here is your help.*

A clink of something metal falling to the floor sounded and the amulet stopped weighing so much to Luce. Luce reached out and picked up the medallion. There was a symbol on it that looked similar to one he had seen while reading up on portals. This medallion could be used to close a portal that had been opened some place it was not supposed to be opened. Luce did not understand why that would be given to him, but started to get to his feet.

"What happened?" Driscoll asked, "Did you trip?"

"No," Luce answered, "I got us some help, but I do not know what help it will be."

"What is that?" Lord Salisbury asked pointing to the medallion that he could barely see in the light."

"The help, I think," Luce answered, "In my reading, I saw this design. It is carved into thingsused to close portals that are opened in wrong places. The person takes the object and goes through the portal, which closes behind them."

"That might explain how the madman appeared one day with anyone knowing from where," Driscoll said, "We will know as soon as we go into this door. Are we ready?"

"I think so," Luce answered as he put the medallion in his pocket. Everyone got their weapons ready before Driscoll pushed the door open.

The room on the other side of the door was lit with red light glowing from the floor. It took up most of the area on this level. The windows were on the other side of the room from the door. There were two levels with three black thrones; two on the one level and the third on the top level. The thrones on the lower level had two identical men sitting on them. The man on the top throne was older, but looked similar to the younger men. Behind the top throne was a portal swirling with silvers and reds.

"Marlon?" Driscoll's voice was almost too quiet for Luce to hear. Driscoll was looking back and forth between the younger men. The two young men must have been the ones who visited the kingdom and wandered places they should not have. They were also the ones who likely stole the wizard's skull. Luce looked around, but did not see it at first. He finally located it on the floor behind the chair the older man, who appeared to be getting some power from it.

"Marlon and Kenji," the older man said, "Welcome our guests. They are here to get rid of us from this land we are claiming as our own."

"We have met this group," the younger man on the left said.

"We have no fear from this group," the younger man on the right said.

"We will deal with them," the older man said as he stood up. Luce prepared himself for the older man's magical attack, while the rest brought their weapons up.

The older man spread his hands out and pushed toward the group. Luce recognized the dueling spell and was able to put up a blocking spell before it hit. His spell did not cover the rest of the group, so the rest were pushed back to the wall. They could not move away from there. Luce responded with a dueling spell that was supposed to paralyze the older man. The older man was able to block the spell and tossed one in response. Driscoll and his group dove to either side and out of the way of this next spell.

Luce and the older man threw dueling spells at each other as everyone else stayed out of the way. The two younger men stayed in their seats and watched the duel, but Driscoll and his group went around the area affected by the spells. They went around and toward the two younger men, who were absorbed in watching the duel. Only when Driscoll attacked the one on the right did the younger men notice the group and started defending themselves. Driscoll and Lord Salisbury attacked the one on the right. Tarak and Wyman attacked the one on the left. The younger men used swords against the swords of the group.

The young men were strong and practiced with swords. They had no trouble defending themselves against two opponents. Tarak and Wyman used the standard methods taught to the guards around the castle, which was meant for fighting against another army of men. The young man was using more sophisticated moves, which was best at keeping the two guards at a distance but not much else. The fight was attacking and blocking with very few hits being exchanged.

Driscoll and Lord Salisbury were doing a little better against the other young man, who was a similar skill level as his twin. Driscoll was the stronger fighter in battle. Lord Salisbury was keeping up, but he knew little more than the guards as far as fighting. The younger man might have defeated him if they had been fighting each other. Driscoll was not only experienced in the fighting style used by the younger man, but also the best one to counter it. He managed to get some hits in on the younger man while still remaining unhurt and keeping Lord Salisbury from being injured.

Luce barely saw the two fights on each side of the room as his energy was being drained by the exchange of dueling spells with the older man. If it had not been for the amulet, Luce would have lost in a short amount of time. The older man's spells had started out as fairly easy dueling spells, but as the battle continued he was using more and more powerful ones. He also never used the same spell twice. Luce had long since run out of spells and was reusing ones as he could. His spells were not quite as powerful, making him dodge more than he would like. He had started weaving spells together in his mind to make them more powerful, but it also made them more unstable. Luce was very lucky none of them blew up until they were closer to the older man. The older man just brushed off the explosions as if they were nothing, but irritants. He would then fire back a stronger spell and Luce would have to dodge.

Wyman lost his sword and Tarak barely saved him from being impaled on the end of the younger man's sword. Tarak fought with the younger man from several minutes as Wyman recovered. Tarak was just about to be pushed back when Wyman skipped retrieving his sword and went into the fight with both arms swinging. The younger man was surprised as the change and had the sword removed from his hand before he could recover. Wyman did not give him time to get the sword back, instead just kept swinging. The younger man brought up his own fists, but the size difference between them and the apparent more experience Wyman had at brawling meant the younger man was at a disadvantage. Tarak stayed back and at ready to help if Wyman needed it.

On the other side of the room, Driscoll was forcing the younger man back with each attack. The younger man fought for all his worth to try and keep pressing forward. Lord Salisbury had been knocked to one side, but was sitting there and trying to get his head back into the fight. The younger man backed toward the portal, but Driscoll was not letting him go so easily. He knocked him to one side to keep him on this level. The younger man got up and attacked Driscoll. Driscoll expected it and blocked it, but the younger man did manage to scrap the tip of his sword across Driscoll's face. Lord Salisbury rejoined the fight and the younger man did his best to fight off both of them.

Luce was throwing every spell he could at the older man and nothing seemed to hurt him, or get close. The amulet felt almost like it was running out of energy. Luce knew he was losing and that if he could not defeat the mad man, none of the group was leaving this place. He needed to find another strategy to fight this man with, but he was having trouble thinking.

"Saint Onan, help me," Luce whispered as he used another blocking spell. This spell was barely enough to keep Luce alive and not affected by the magic. There did not seem to be an immediate answer. The older men threw another spell before Luce had a chance to think up one to throw back. Luce dodged it and ended up lying on the floor. As he got to his feet, Luce felt a surge of energy go through him and a spell came to his mind that he had never heard of before. Luce used it before the older man could attack him again. The older man put up his blocking spell barely in time to avoid being hit by the spell. The older man looked concerned this time and hesitated on his attack for half a second. Luce attacked before the older man could do anything. The older man blocked it.

The younger men were quickly losing and backing up. They moved up to the next level.

"Father," the younger man on the left said, "I believe we should try this another time and another way."

"Perhaps you are right," the older man said. He took an extra several seconds to prepare his next spell. Luce put up a strong blocking spell to ready himself for the attack.

The spell slammed into Luce's chest despite the

blocking spell. It lifted him off his feet and sent him backwards at a high rate of speed. Luce smashed into the wall and fell to the floor. There was a crunch when he hit and pain shot through his whole side. He tried to move, but found he could not.

The older man headed toward the portal. Driscoll and the rest of the group were doing what they could to back the three toward the portal. They were winning, but Luce was sure that if they sent the men through the portal the men would just find some way to get back through somewhere else. Someone had to go through the portal and seal it with the medallion.

Luce tried to move, but too many things were broken. He managed to get a hand free and into his pocket. The medallion was right there and he was able to grab it. Luce tried to think of a way to get to the portal just after the men had been pushed through. There did not seem to be any way to do it. Something tugged on the medallion and Luce looked down. Sandra had grabbed the medallion and was trying to take it away. Luce could do nothing, other than let go.

Sandra flew with the medallion toward Driscoll. He grabbed it when she was able to get close enough. The men were pushed through the portal and Driscoll held up the medallion as he followed them through. There was a bright light before anyone else could get close enough to follow him and they all had to turn away. When the light disappeared, the portal was gone. Everyone was silent as they stared at where the portal and Driscoll had vanished.

The red light slowly disappeared as the spell dissipated, but rather than everything going dark, sun came in through the window. The sunlight hit the stain glass of the cathedral windows and created patterns on the cream coloured walls. No one spoke or moved for several minutes. A cough tickled Luce's throat as he lay there until he could not hold it in any longer. The noise startled everyone out of their trance.

They looked at each other and put their weapons away.

"Do you think he is still alive?" Lord Salisbury asked.

"For a short amount of time," Luce coughed slightly as he used his good hand to dig into his bag, "They may kill him right away, or they might just capture him. I do not know because I do not know what is on the other side of the portal."

"Is there any way to get there?" Tarak asked.

"I do not know," Luce answered, "That is a question for Nava, when we get back there."

"It did not take long to get here from there," Lord Salisbury said, "It should not take long to get back." He and the two guards came down to where Luce was lying.

"Can you move?" Tarak asked.

"In a few minutes," Luce answered, "What happened to Sandra?" The three looked around, but none of them saw the fairy.

"She was nowhere near the portal," Lord Salisbury said.

"She threw the medallion to Driscoll and then disappeared," Luce said, "Maybe she decided everything was finished and she wanted to go home."

"Was she able to do that?" Tarak asked.

"She has her own magic," Luce answered. His hand found the bottle he was looking for and brought it out.

"What is that?" Lord Salisbury asked.

"A healing potion," Luce answered, "It was given to me when we got the food in the forest." He took the top of the bottle and brought it to his lips. He poured the liquid into his mouth. It had no taste, but his body was sure that it did not want it.

"That was why my arm healed so quickly," Lord Salisbury said.

"Yes," Luce said once he had swallowed. His body started to burn and he had to put the bottle down. He started to shake as he continued to heat up. The others stepped away from him. Luce continued to shake as smoke came from him. It seemed like he was close to going up in flames, but just before his body reached that, he stopped shaking and fell unconscious.

THE JOURNEY BACK TO THE PORTAL AND THEN BACK TO PROSTER.

Luce woke to find the others sitting there watching him. He tried to sit up, but found it too painful. Every bone that had been broken was screaming in pain.

"How long was I out?" Luce asked.

"Half an hour," Lord Salisbury answered, "It does not appear the healing potion has finished working."

"I cannot move yet," Luce said, "But as soon as I can we can leave. Has anyone come to find out what happened?"

"No," Lord Salisbury answered, "I do not believe you should have drunk so much of the healing potion."

"I also should not have drunk it straight," Luce replied, "But I wanted it to work faster. We should be packed up and ready to go as soon as I can move."

"We are packed up," Lord Salisbury said, "And ready to go."

"I need to wizard's skull from behind the top chair," Luce said, "It needs to be buried properly with the rest of the skeleton from the highest tower of the castle in Proster."

"I will get it," Wyman said getting to his feet.

"Be careful," Lord Salisbury said.

Wyman walked over to the chair and picked up the skull. Nothing happened to him and he walked back to them. Wyman placed the skull beside Luce before sitting back down where he had been before. Luce used his good hand to pack it and the bottle of healing potion into his bag.

Luce was sure he could feel the bones knit back together and it was painful. He kept trying to move to see if he could. It was slow and made Luce more impatient. Finally he move somewhat, so Luce stood up. His legs wanted to give out, but he kept on his feet. The rest moved much slower and looked concerned about him moving, but none of them said anything about waiting.

Luce picked up his pack and started for the door. The rest followed. They left the cathedral. Outside the sun had come out and the darkness was gone. The crows were also gone and the city did not look abandoned anymore, but looked ready for the people to move back in. The group left the city and went back across the field, which was now green and not dead at all. They went through the forest. The forest was now full of life.

By the time they reached the other side of the forest night had fallen. Luce was still limping, but otherwise he was healed. They made up camp and fell asleep shortly after having something to eat.

Luce woke to the sun rising. He looked around and saw that everyone else was still asleep. Luce could feel pain along his left leg. He went through his cloak until he found the bottle of healing potion and pulled it out. After taking a sip, he put it back. There was no tingling to tell Luce if the healing was happening, but he did not move for several minutes anymore. The pain did not go away. Luce decided to get up and start breakfast.

He got started with gathering wood for the fire. By the time he had the fire going, Tarak and Wyman were awake. They helped to get the rest of breakfast together. When they were done, Lord Salisbury was woken up so they could all eat. When they were finished, Tarak and Wyman cleaned up. Then they came back to sit around the fire.

"What do we do now?" Wyman asked.

"We need to get back to the Nava and see what she can do to get King Driscoll back," Lord Salisbury answered, "We need to get him back and head for Proster."

"We need to find Nastaran," Luce said, "Without her it will take weeks to get back and then everything will be harder to fix."

"If you had not come to Proster with this whole idea, none of this would have happened," Lord Salisbury said.

"It had never been my intention for Driscoll to come with me," Luce said, "I had hoped he would just give me the information and let me go on my own. How do you turn down a king who wants to do something? I know your answer because Driscoll came along despite your better judgement."

"I worked hard to get him to stay," Lord Salisbury said, "If you had said anything to discourage him, he would not have decided to come. All you had to say was no."

"Then maybe you should have let me know that," Luce said, "So, I knew it was possible. I assumed he would be talked out of it by his advisors and it would not be my responsibility. I do not live at court anymore, which means I do not deal with politics on a regular basis. Nor do I live in Proster and know the situation there. I learned a small amount in the short time I was there, but nothing on the fact that Driscoll wanted a break. So, next time send me a message to let me know I should tell the king no when he requests traveling with me."

"How do we find Nastaran?" Tarak asked before Lord Salisbury could say anything, "She left us here and headed back without saying how to find her after we defeated the men."

"I do not know," Luce answered, "She did not say anything about it. We can try calling her and hope she can hear us."

"I cannot think of a better idea," Tarak shrugged. He got to his feet and oriented himself so his back is to the forest and he was facing the direction she had gone.

"Nastaran," Tarak shouted. He waited several minutes for any kind of response.

"Nastaran," Tarak was louder this time. Everyone was quiet as they waited for a response.

"Nastaran!" Tarak screamed. There still was no response. Tarak gave up and came back to sit beside the fire.

"Are other ideas?" Tarak's voice was rough.

"We can start walking," Luce said, "And hope she finds us when people figure out the men are gone."

"Then we should pack up," Lord Salisbury got to his feet. Tarak and Wyman got up and started packing as well. Luce made sure the fire was out before joining them.

They packed up and starting moving. They made good progress despite Luce's new limp, but it was much slower than their pace to get to the area. They saw much more of the scenery this time. At noon they stopped for lunch.

It was a brief break before they were getting back to their feet. Just as they were about to continue on when they saw someone coming down the path toward them. Tarak and Wyman started to draw their swords when the person was close enough to recognize Nastaran. She was in front of them in no time.

"We were not sure how to find you," Luce said, "So, we started walking."

"I am sorry I am late," Nastaran said, "But I was distracted when word got back that the mad man was gone from this world. Where are the other two?"

"They got sucked into the portal that took the mad man away," Lord Salisbury answered, "And we need to figure out how to get them back."

"I am uncertain how to go about that," Nastaran said, "We need to get back to Nava and ask her what can be done."

"Then let us go," Lord Salisbury said.

Nastaran turned around and the men followed her.

It took about a day for the group to arrive back in the field. They reached the circle where they had been brought to this world and stopped to rest. Nastaran disappeared. A moment passed before Nava appeared in the field with them. She looked them over for a minute. None of the group said anything.

"Word has reached me that the madman is gone," Nava said, "For which I thank you."

"They went through a portal," Luce said, "They could come back any time."

"They have not come back yet," Nava said, "And now that I know how they got here, I can keep them out."

"King Driscoll went through with them to close the portal," Lord Salisbury said, "Is there anything we can do to rescue him?"

"I do not know where that portal goes," Nava said, "Nor can I open a portal to that place. King Driscoll is lost to us unless he finds a way of coming back from there."

"Then I must get back to Proster with the news as soon as possible," Lord Salisbury said, "Prince Hillel will need to be informed as to what happened to his father and preparations to crown him will need to be started."

"I can send you back," Nava said.

"Just a moment," Luce said. Nava turned to him.

"Yes?" Nava asked.

"I came looking for answer to a mystery and I do not want to go back without the answer," Luce said, "Some years ago the magic disappeared from Proster and the kingdoms surrounding it. It has made things difficult for wizards such as me because the energy disappeared with it. Any magical creatures caught in that world suffer from the same problem. Sandra was just about killed because of it. What caused this?"

"It is likely the effect of the portal being closed," Nava answered, "To avoid any dangerous creatures from going through the portal, I closed shortly after I became the portal guardian. Closing it keeps the magic and the magical energy on this side of the portal. That is where the magic went."

"Is it possible to keep the portal open a small amount so some energy gets through?" Luce asked, "Because there are still some magical creatures caught on the other side. Also spellcasters need the energy as well."

"There is a way I can keep the portal open only a small amount," Nava said, "But should word get out that the portal is open again, creatures that should not will be trying to get through the portal. I will try to be extra vigilant, but all of you must never speak of the portal again."

"I am all right with that," Luce said.

"I need to tell them what happened to Driscoll," Lord Salisbury said, "I cannot do that if you wish us never to speak of the portal again."

"It might be better if they did not know the exact details anyway," Luce said, "Most people do not believe in magic and to know such a thing exists would cause more problems. They do not truly need to know exactly what happened. We just tell them Driscoll will not be returning to his kingdom and he wants his son to be crowned. After that, we do not tell anyone anything."

Lord Salisbury stared at Luce as he thought about it. Tarak and Wyman did not seem to disagree with Luce's argument.

"No one must ever be told about the portal, or where Driscoll is," Nava said, "You must all take oaths to never say anything about the portal."

"I swear," Luce said.

"As do I," Tarak said.

"I will never tell anyone," Wyman said.

"I do not completely agree with it," Lord Salisbury said, "But I also swear never to talk about it."

"Good," Nava said, "I would suggest you head straight for the road once you are through the portal. Getting lost in that forest can mean you are never seen again."

"So, we have found out," Lord Salisbury said, "We did not have a map and wandered the circle of the forest for several days. We did not go along the road, nor did we know that it was possible."

"I will give you a map so that you can get home safe," Nava said. She disappeared and the group found themselves standing in the clearing in the forest with their horses still tied to the tree.

Nava reappeared with a scroll in her hand.

"Here is the map," she offered it to Lord Salisbury, "Also know that time moves differently on the other side of the portal. You have lived through days, but here a mere minute has past."

"There is one more thing that I almost forgot," Luce said, "Sandra disappeared after the portal closed. I hope she made it home."

"I doubt she did," Nava said, "Fairy magic is different from human and things happen to them that does not happen to humans in the same situation. She would not have just disappeared if she was headed home. She would have more likely stuck around until a better time to leave and fly home arrived. Since she disappeared shortly after the portal closed it is likely she was sucked through in the magic it took to close it."

"Then she is in trouble," Luce said.

"Fairies are hardy and are powerful in their own way," Nava said, "I would suggest she will be fine and will do what she can to get home."

Luce nodded.

"I bid you good luck," Nava said before disappearing.

The group stood there for a moment before going to their horses. Lord Salisbury took the reins of Driscoll's horse as well as his own. They followed the map through the forest to the road. It was a much shorter route than they had found to get to the portal. It took less than a day before they were riding along the road toward the city.

Lord Salisbury and the guards were quiet as they rode. Luce did not disturb them. He understood they were mourning the loss of their king and friend. He knew it was his fault Driscoll was gone. Somewhere he had known taking Driscoll had been a bad idea, but there was never any point when it seemed Luce could have talked Driscoll out of coming. Luce supposed Driscoll had been his friend and a loss in his life as well. The others might have felt better if Luce had gone off instead of coming with them to the city, but he did not want to desert them when it was possible they might need him.

It was close to time for supper when they reached the city. They made their silent procession through the city and back up to the castle. People looked up at them, but no one really paid attention to them. However, word must have reached the castle before they did because Hillel, Weldon, and Rana were standing in the court yard waiting for them. Luce barely noticed the men, because his attention was on Rana. She looked them over and then searched out each of their eyes. Luce found himself looking at the stones of the court yard, as did the others, but he still saw her understanding and tears start before she went inside. Weldon also seemed to understand, but said and did nothing.

The group stopped in front of Hillel and Lord Salisbury dismounted. He bowed to Hillel before giving the news in a low voice. Luce barely paid attention as his mind went to what Rana was going through. Driscoll had promised he would come back, but had made his sacrifice so the rest could return. Likely he did not think about the ones who would miss him, but instead assumed his kingdom was in good hands.

Hillel bowed his head at the sad news that his father would not be returning, but without knowledge of life or death. There were no tears, or difficulty like Rana. He just stood there for a minute before moving on to the next thing that needed to be dealt with. Luce knew he would bring up his coronation as soon as he thought he could without it seeming inappropriate, but he would wait until that moment.

Luce went with Tarak and Wyman to the stables to help with the horses before finding the castle steward. He found a room had already been made up for him. There was no comments about when he was leaving, but the castle steward gave no indication Hillel cared whether he stayed or not.

Over the next several days, what little of the story they could tell was given to the court and they were questioned about it by everyone. They said nothing as they had sworn. Luce dealt with the wizard's body and making sure all of the wizard was buried together. Then he spent some time trying to figure out what he was going to do next.

Luce was wandering the castle with no particular place in mind. He had been up to the tower. Everything had been cleaned out of it now. All that were left was markings on the walls no one could remove. Hillel did not seem bothered that the room was empty, nor did he seem to have any plans for it. Luce had briefly thought about asking if he could move in, but he had seen enough of Hillel for the idea to hold no appeal.

Luce had wandered to the balcony and looked out over the court yard and the little that could be seen of the city. It was quiet almost like the quiet before the storm. Except no one was expecting a storm, they were just mourning the loss of a good king. A king for the people.

"Are you not cold out here?" Rana's voice came from behind Luce.

"A little bit," Luce said turning to her. She had a shawl wrapped around her for warmth. It had frozen enough in the kingdom that the trees had lost their leaves and everyone had switched to warmer clothes. Luce had left his cloak in his room, but his power had kept him from really noticing the cold.

"Hillel is going to make his announcement from here tomorrow," Rana said coming to the railing.

"Is he going to do the full coronation?" Luce asked.

"In two weeks," Rana answered, "Weldon convinced him to give the people some time to mourn for Driscoll."

"That is good," Luce said.

"Is he really dead?" Rana asked.

"I cannot answer that," Luce answered. Rana nodded but her expression was showed she was hurting. Luce wanted to ease the pain, but he could not tell her what would help. He looked out over the city again and his mind went back to a different king, the one who would look out over the city with longing in his face and fear in his heart.

Rana took his hand in hers. Luce glanced at her, but she was focused out over the city as well.

"They are really going to miss him," Rana said.

"We all are," Luce answered. They stood there for a few more minutes. Luce started to feel cold and he glanced at Rana to notice that she was shivering.

"Come on, let us go back inside and warm up," Luce said tugging gently on Rana's hand. She smiled at Luce and let him pull her inside the castle. It was slightly warmer.

'What about you?" Rana asked, "Where are you going to do?"

"I have not decided what to do yet," Luce answered, "But if I do not find a direction by the time the snow falls I will have to stay for the winter."

"Then I guess you are here for the winter," Rana said as she smiled and pointed out the window in the door. Luce looked out and found the first snowflakes of the season falling from the sky. He smiled and looked back to Rana. Luce pulled her close and Rana pressed her lips to his.

CONCLUSION, OR IS IT?

Mitchell closed the book. His finished his drink and sat quietly. The fire was starting to burn down again. He did not move to put another log on it, or even put the book back in the box. He thought over the story.

It had to be fiction. Did it not? None of this could be real. This was not history, but someone's stories. His history had nothing to do with these stories. These men and these kings had never existed.

Noises came from somewhere in the house. It sounded like the servants were starting their day. Starting the fire in the stove, gathering everything to start breakfast, and straightening anything that had not been dealt with the night before. The real world, the non-magical world. The world where these books were fiction and he had an appointment this morning. He should be getting ready for that appointment, but the next book was calling for him.

Mitchell sighed as he got to his feet. He had to live life in this world, the real one. So, he might as well get started. He took the book back to the box. He put it in, but brought the next one out at the same time. The leather was soft, the pages wonderful, and the book felt right in his hand.

Mitchell found himself easing back into his chair. The fire gave just enough light to read by as he opened it.

ABOUT THE AUTHOR

Heather Mantler is a lover of fairy tales and fables. She is also a student of psychology. She lives in Prince George, British Columbia and is a member of the writing group Scribblers Unanimous. Heather is always working on another story as she hopes to finish every story idea that she has ever written down. She was a nominee for the fiction category of the 2012 Prince George Regional Arts and Cultural Awards and short listed for the 2013 John Harris Fiction Awards.

Heather encourages her readers to post their reviews on Amazon.com or Good Reads.